LIFE IN THE WOODS

B.E. Russell

XCEL
PUBLISHING

CONTENTS

LIFE IN THE WOODS

1

WINTER'S QUIET EMBRACE

George woke to the hush of a new snowfall before dawn, the only sound a soft crackle from the banked embers in his woodstove. The glow of the dying fire bathed the logs of his cabin in flickering orange, lending a comforting warmth against the deep cold of a northern winter. He sat up slowly, muscles stiff from another night in his old bunk, and stretched his arms overhead. Outside, the wind gusted, sifting snow crystals through the tall pines that surrounded his little refuge on the edge of the lake. It sounded like a distant whisper, a gentle hush that seemed to say *stay inside a little longer, let the day begin on its own time.* But George had learned, over many years, that the woods waited for no one. If he lingered too long in bed, the day's chores would pile up, like the drifts forming just beyond his threshold.

He scratched the thick gray beard that covered his chin and cheeks—an unruly marker of his years spent in this remote northern country—and swung his legs off the bed. His first order of business was to stoke the stove and add fresh firewood, ensuring the cabin would remain warm when he finally bundled up to face the outdoors. The iron door of the stove squeaked on its hinges as he pulled it open, revealing a bed of orange coals, dotted with glowing embers. With practiced efficiency, George laid on a few small sticks of split birch until they caught flame, then added heavier pieces of maple and oak. Before long, the fire was crackling steadily, its radiant heat seeping out into the cabin's single main room.

While the fire built up strength, George shambled over to his modest kitchen corner, which consisted of a weathered wooden counter and a handful of cabinets. His tin coffee pot and percolator waited by the sink, so he filled the pot with water from a large jug he kept thawed near the stove. He set the pot on a metal trivet atop the woodstove and measured out spoons of coarse coffee grounds. The smell of coffee, once heated, would filter throughout the cabin, mixing with the smell of burning wood and pine sap—a comforting morning bouquet he'd grown to cherish.

He tugged on a thick wool sweater and layered over it a flannel shirt, then padded across the plank floor to the small window beside his bed. The glass was clouded by a delicate lace of frost, but through it, he could see the darkness thinning on the horizon. The clouds had parted enough for a hint of moonlight earlier, and now the faint glow of pre-dawn light revealed freshly fallen snow piled high along the edge of the lake. George wondered if the water had frozen fully overnight. Yesterday, only the shallow edges had been sealed in ice. If the cold snap had persisted, there was a good chance the entire surface would be stable enough for his first real venture onto the ice. Excitement stirred in him at the thought of drilling a hole, dropping a line, and perhaps pulling up a Lake Trout for dinner. Ice fishing was one of his greatest winter pleasures—quiet, solitary, requiring both patience and hope.

But first, breakfast. Once the coffee began to gently percolate, George rummaged through a small tin of rolled oats, measuring out enough for a single bowl. He added a pinch of salt, some dried cranberries, and a bit of sugar before setting a pot of water on the stove to boil. While he waited, he kept busy by turning to the stack of logs he had brought in the day before. He methodically inspected them, selecting those best suited to feed the stove throughout the day. Chopping wood was part of his everyday routine, but it demanded attention all the same. Without a steady supply of dry, seasoned wood, the cabin would lose its cozy sanctuary feel in a matter of hours.

Outside, the wind rattled the eaves, and a fine swirl of snow dusted the narrow windowsill. George reached for his coffee cup—an old enamel mug chipped around the rim—and poured himself the first brew of the day. Bitter and strong, it instantly chased away the last vestiges of sleep. He sipped slowly, aware that simple rituals like this formed the foundation of his life in the woods: a warm stove, fresh coffee, an honest day's work. He was never short on gratitude.

When his oats finished cooking, George sat down at his small wooden table, the only table in the cabin, which he had built by hand years ago. The table bore countless nicks and scratches, each one a tiny memory of meals past, gear repairs, or nights spent tying flies for the upcoming fishing season. He ate unhurriedly. There was no point in rushing in a place where time ran according to the rhythms of nature, where the sun and the season itself dictated most daily schedules. Outside, the day would reveal itself in due course.

After breakfast, he layered up. Thick woolen socks, lined pants, a heavy coat, and his sturdy snow boots. He then moved to his small workbench by the front door, where he kept his hat, gloves, and scarf. The bench was cluttered with various items: an old camera, a battered fishing net, a jar of paintbrushes from his plein air outings—none of which he'd be using today, at least not until the snow stopped swirling.

He stepped outside, and the cold rushed to greet him, sharp against his cheeks. His breath formed small puffs in the air. The morning light was weak, but it caught the surface of the snow, making the entire landscape sparkle like crushed diamonds. George took a moment to simply stand there, letting the hush of the forest settle around him. No distant hum of traffic, no clamor of human voices. Just the faint whistle of the wind and the gentle creaks of tall pines under the weight of snow.

Looking to the horizon, he could see the sky begin to pale with the promise of sunrise. The dark silhouette of the tree line stood quietly against that ever-brightening canvas. A sense of peace washed over him. He often reminded himself that these moments were the reason he had chosen to make his life here: the profound stillness, the unhurried bond with the natural world. He was not a recluse by temperament, but solitude fed his spirit in ways he had never known when he was younger.

He ventured around the side of the cabin to where his woodpile was stacked beneath a sloping roof extension. The snowfall was slightly deeper than yesterday, maybe six or seven inches of new powder. He tested it with his boots—fresh, light, and perfect for snowshoeing later in the day. For now, he grabbed his axe from its hook. The wooden handle was smooth from long use. He had replaced the old handle just last year, a task requiring patience to fit the wedge properly, but now it felt perfectly balanced in his hands.

The chore of chopping firewood was almost meditative to George. He carried a half dozen logs from the pile, setting them onto the chopping block. With precise swings, he split each round into halves or quarters, depending on the thickness. The steady *thwack* of steel on wood reverberated across the clearing. Every so often, he paused to watch tiny clouds of breath escape his mouth, or to listen for stirring animals in the woods. Chickadees flitted among the snow-laden branches, chirping cheerily despite the frigid temperatures. Their little voices added a bright note to the morning quiet.

Once he had chopped a sufficient stack for the rest of the day, he neatly stacked it in his covered rack to keep it dry. He brushed snow from his gloves and turned back to the cabin, arms full of split wood. Already, the smell of fresh coffee and the lingering warmth from the stove beckoned him to return inside. But before stepping in, George gazed out at the lake. He could see where the ice reached from the shore to a few dozen yards out, an opaque white that blended with the snowfall. Further out, the center of the lake looked darker, suggesting that the freeze was not yet complete.

Inside, he set the fresh firewood by the stove, then took a moment to remove his gloves and warm his hands over the flickering flames behind the stove's grate. The cabin was still not fully heated, but it was far more comfortable than the biting cold outside. He set his axe against the wall near the door—an easy place to grab it if he needed more wood split later. All the while, the winter morning pressed on, with the sky growing lighter by the minute.

Given the uncertain thickness of the ice, George decided that a walk through the woods would be safer than attempting to venture too far out onto the lake. At least until midday, when he could test the ice more thoroughly. So, he grabbed his snowshoes from their hooks on the wall. They were traditional wooden frames with rawhide lacing, something he cherished for their craftsmanship and reliability. Modern ones might be lighter or more compact, but George found a certain poetry in using handmade gear that connected him to centuries of explorers, trappers, and natives who had traversed these lands long before him.

He strapped them on carefully, adjusting the leather bindings around his boots, and stepped back outside, gently planting his poles in the snow to maintain his balance. The air had grown marginally brighter, though the sun was still hidden behind a flat, gray bank of clouds. Snow continued to drift down, not in thick flakes, but in a soft, steady dusting that veiled the woods.

His first steps into the deeper drifts around the side of the cabin made him thankful for the snowshoes. Each footfall felt like a buoyant press on the powder rather than a sinking struggle. The pines around him, laden with white, stood as silent guardians. Their branches sagged under the weight but did not break—a testament to their resilience. George began his walk, heading northward along a gentle slope that overlooked the lake. He moved slowly, scanning for tracks, signs of animal activity, or any subtle changes in the environment. This was a daily practice—part curiosity, part stewardship of the land that provided for him.

Before long, he spotted the distinct trail of a snowshoe hare hopping from one clump of shrubs to another. Tiny paw prints, fresh and crisp, told him the hare was no more than an hour ahead of him. He crouched low, following the trail with his eyes until it disappeared into a dense thicket. Further along, at the base of a fir tree, he discovered tracks of a fox—long, narrow prints, in almost a straight line. The fox had likely been hunting for the hare or for mice scurrying beneath the snow. Such observations were an endless source of fascination for George: a drama playing out each day, unseen yet fully present, the forest a vast stage for countless small players.

He pressed on, following a gentle ridge that curved along the lakeshore. The vantage point offered a panoramic view of the water, which indeed appeared partially frozen. The wind had swept the middle of the lake more fiercely, preventing the snow from settling evenly. Patches of exposed ice formed dark, glistening sheets amid swirling flurries. George paused to watch a small flock of crows flying across the sky, cawing loudly as they headed toward the stands of old-growth pines on the far side of the lake. From this vantage, the cabin looked like part of the landscape—little more than a bump of logs and a thin trail of chimney smoke rising into the still morning air.

Continuing his hike, he took time to appreciate the subtle variations of winter's palette: the faint purples and blues in the snow's shadows, the emerald green of spruce boughs, the gentle browns and grays of hardwoods stripped bare of leaves. Occasionally, a breeze would stir the branches overhead, showering him in a fine spray of powder. He'd pause, remove a glove, and use his bare fingers to brush the snow from his beard. The cold stung, but in a bracing, enlivening way.

Eventually, the path led him to a small clearing where he sometimes collected fallen branches for kindling. The clearing opened up just enough for a clear line of sight into the forest interior. To his surprise, he noticed something large and dark move between the trees on the far side—a Moose, most likely. With careful steps, George quietly approached the edge of the clearing, wanting a better glimpse. There, partially concealed by a cluster of birch trunks, stood a majestic bull Moose, head bowed to nibble at low-hanging branches. Its breath came in visible puffs, and its thick winter coat blended well with the subdued forest tones. George felt a thrill of awe. Even after years in these woods, such an encounter always struck him as a minor miracle. The bull Moose was unaware of George's presence, or if it was, it paid no mind, absorbed in the simple task of finding breakfast. George watched for several minutes in hushed silence, hardly daring to move. Finally, the Moose lifted its head, revealing the broad muzzle and a proud set of antlers that would soon be shed. Their eyes briefly met—man and beast acknowledging each other's presence across a short distance but in vastly different worlds. Then, with a turn of its heavy head, the Moose ambled deeper into the forest.

George stood still, heart pounding with quiet excitement. Moments like these, fleeting and unplanned, reaffirmed his devotion to living here—where the boundary between human and animal existence felt thinner, more permeable, where each day brought the possibility of wordless communion with creatures that roamed freely. He exhaled a frosty breath, whispered a silent thanks, and turned back toward the direction of his cabin.

By the time he returned home, the day had advanced enough that the interior of the cabin was comfortably warm. He shed his heavy winter coat and boots by the door, propping his snowshoes against the wall to dry. His nose was still cold to the touch, but a contented glow filled him. From the window, he could see that the light snowfall was continuing. He might not make it out onto the lake for ice fishing that afternoon, but that was alright— he had plenty of days ahead. Winter was a companion he knew intimately.

George set about tidying the small space. Living in the cabin required a certain discipline to keep everything in its proper place; clutter was the enemy of tranquility. He folded his blankets, straightened his fly-tying desk, and washed his oatmeal pot in a small basin with water warmed from the stove. As he cleaned, he glanced over at the bookshelf, which held a few treasured volumes: some field guides on birds and mammals, a handful of philosophical texts he liked to revisit in the evenings, and well-worn fishing manuals. He considered reading for a bit, but something else beckoned first: his journal.

Pulling out a leather-bound notebook from a sturdy wooden chest, he settled by the fireplace. The notebook's pages were thick and slightly yellowed, each filled with his careful handwriting— notes, sketches, thoughts, and observations collected over months and years. The entries ranged from the mundane (the day's temperature, a list of chores) to the deeply introspective (reflections on solitude, on mortality, on the subtle changes in the forest ecosystem). This morning's events deserved a fresh entry. He dipped his pen in a small inkwell and began to write:

January 3rd, dawn. Woke to a quiet snowfall, about six inches new by my measure. Coffee and oatmeal warmed me through. Ventured northward around the lake—beautiful hush in the woods. Spotted tracks of hare and fox. Saw a bull Moose in the clearing. A majestic sight; we observed each other for a moment. Too early for ice fishing, but soon. This is why I live here: for moments like the one with the Moose, where words are unnecessary, and a sense of belonging runs deep.

He continued writing for several pages, describing the crispness of the air, the color of the sky, and how the cabin felt especially cozy upon returning. He sketched a quick outline of the Moose, capturing the slope of its neck and the shape of its antlers. Though not an artist by training, he enjoyed leaving these small drawings in his journal, each one a memory he could revisit whenever he wished.

Once he finished, he closed the journal and set it aside, letting the ink dry. He rose and moved to the small table where he kept his fly-tying vise and materials. Winter was the perfect time to stockpile new flies for the coming seasons. Even if the fish under the ice had no need for those delicate imitations of insects, he would be ready by spring and summer, when the trout and bass rose eagerly to the surface. He sorted through colored feathers, bits of fur, and spools of thread until he found the right materials for a pattern he had been experimenting with—something that mimicked a fat caddis fly. With deft fingers, he clamped a hook in place and began winding bright thread around it. The process required focus and a gentle hand; tying too fast or too tightly could ruin the delicate balance of the fly. He worked in near silence, pausing now and then to sip the last of his coffee, which had grown lukewarm but still tasted good.

Outside, the snow abated slightly, replaced by a subtle hush. Glancing through the window, George noticed that the clouds were thinning—there was a chance for a bit of pale sunlight before day's end. He finished tying one fly, clipped the thread, and examined his work. It looked serviceable, though he might need to tweak the pattern. That was part of the fun: the experimentation, the hopeful anticipation that this new creation might be the one to fool a wily trout in a hidden stream come April or May.

After tidying his materials, George stood up, stretched, and checked the time on his old wind-up pocket watch. Still mid-morning. Perfect for a short foray onto the lake—at least to test the ice. He laced up his boots again and donned his coat, but this time he replaced the snowshoes with a sturdy pair of ice cleats that could strap onto his soles. He grabbed his ice chisel, a long steel rod with a chiseled end, used for probing the thickness of the ice near shore.

Stepping outside, he was met by an almost eerie calm. The snowfall had ceased, leaving behind an untouched blanket of white. Thin beams of sunlight began to break through the clouds, illuminating the lake's surface. George walked carefully to the edge of the shoreline, each step sending a faint crunch through the snow. At the transition from land to lake, he tested the ice with his chisel. It made a solid, echoing *thud*. He chipped away to measure its thickness. Two inches near the edge—enough to stand on, but not quite the four or five inches he preferred for safe fishing further out. Still, he inched forward, testing each step. The ice held, albeit with a few small cracks singing out in protest. He decided not to push his luck. Another day or two of cold might make it safe enough to set up his tip-ups.

Before turning back, he noticed a set of tracks crossing the ice a short distance from shore. They looked like coyote or possibly fox prints, meandering across the ice and then disappearing near a rocky outcrop. It reminded him that, even in this seemingly barren winter environment, life was always in motion—creatures constantly roamed in search of food, shelter, or simply following their instincts.

With that, George returned to solid ground and made his way along the narrow path back to the cabin. The sun now dipped behind a fleeting cloud, casting elongated shadows over the snow. He felt a small pang of hunger as noon approached. So, once inside, he peeled off his layers, tossed another log into the woodstove, and set about preparing a simple lunch. A can of beans, a piece of salted pork he'd cured himself, and a thick slice of the bread he had baked the week before. It was hearty fare, perfectly suited for staving off the chill of winter. As he cooked, the cabin filled with the savory smell of sizzling pork, intermingling with the last smoky wisps of the morning's fire.

After lunch, he cleaned his plate and utensils, then stretched out on his bunk for a few minutes, listening to the gentle pop of the fire. A midday rest was sometimes all he needed to reset his energy for the second half of the day. Outside, the wind picked up again, rattling the shutter on the north side of the cabin. He made a mental note to secure it better before evening. Even small tasks like tightening shutters, checking for drafts, or brushing excess snow off the roof were crucial in a place where winter's severity demanded constant vigilance.

Despite the renewed wind, George felt compelled to go out one more time, to wander a bit in the direction of the thick pines that sheltered a variety of wildlife. As he rose from the bunk, he slipped a notebook and a pencil into his coat pocket—if he came across anything noteworthy, he wanted to document it immediately. He then strapped on his snowshoes again, stepped out, and locked the cabin door behind him. The air bit at his cheeks, but he welcomed it as a reminder he was alive.

The forest at midday was a curious blend of subdued light and drifting snow. He made his way to the stand of pines, where the canopy was so dense that only a few flakes reached the ground. The earth here was a patchwork of pine needles and shallow snow. He found the place comforting—like a cathedral of tall trunks and soft murmurs. He walked in silence, occasionally resting a gloved hand on a tree trunk as though greeting an old friend. This was the place where, in past winters, he had watched owls perch silently, scanning for voles or mice. Today, he saw only a scattering of small birds, chirping quietly above him.

A short time later, he climbed a low rise, using a trunk for balance. From that vantage point, he could see further into the heart of the pines. Suddenly, he heard it: the distant, mournful howl of a wolf. It echoed through the trees, raising hairs on the back of George's neck. The call was answered by another, then another, forming a haunting chorus. George smiled to himself. Wolves were a testament to the wildness of these woods, a reminder that he shared this land with creatures shaped by an entirely different set of instincts and social bonds.

He waited there, listening until the howls faded into the hush of snow and wind. Then, with careful steps, he made his way back down the rise. The day's light was already starting to shift, a sign that dusk would come early thanks to the heavy cloud cover. George returned to the cabin, his heart full of gratitude for another day spent in the quiet company of the winter woods.

By late afternoon, darkness was creeping in. He lit a lantern on the small table and checked his provisions for dinner. The Lake Trout he'd caught a few days prior was well-stored in a cold box on the shaded side of the cabin, so he decided to thaw it near the stove. He seasoned it with salt, pepper, and a few herbs from a small jar on the shelf. As it cooked, he reflected on the day: the restful morning by the stove, the discovery of fresh tracks, and that magical encounter with the bull Moose. He felt a contentment so deep that, in another life, he might have sought to share it with a crowd of people. But here, in his cabin, the contentment was its own companion.

When the fish finished cooking, George ate slowly. The rich flavor of the trout and the warmth of the stove made him appreciate the land's generosity. After washing up, he settled beside the fireplace with a well-worn copy of a classic nature volume—John Muir's writings, one of his favorites. The pages were yellowed, but the words carried a timeless reverence for wilderness that resonated with George's own experiences. He read until the fire began to die down.

At last, he banked the coals for the night, ensuring they would still be hot when he woke to feed them fresh logs. He made a quick note in his journal about the wind picking up and the forecast he inferred from the clouds. Perhaps a larger storm was coming. He took one final look outside the window, where the moon was faint behind swirling clouds. The forest was dark and still. He said a quiet goodnight to the silent pines, to the lake whose ice would soon be thick enough to fish through, and to the creatures that roamed unseen in the snow.

Then George climbed into his bunk, the thick wool blankets pulled up around his shoulders. The glow from the last embers flickered across the cabin walls. He listened to the wind whistle through the eaves, a lullaby that rose and fell. The logs of the cabin creaked softly, settling into the cold. As he closed his eyes, he felt a deep gratitude for the day that had passed—a day of small wonders, from the Moose in the clearing to the hush of the falling snow. In the morning, he would wake to that same hush, stoke the fire, and greet the winter anew, ready for whatever the woods offered him next. And in this quiet, he found a simple truth: that life, in all its solitary rhythms and gentle comforts, was enough, here in the wintery heart of the north woods.

2

FIRELIGHT REFLECTIONS

George woke the morning after his encounter with the bull Moose, the memory of that massive creature fresh in his mind. Even in the soft glow of daybreak, an impression lingered—Moose breath steaming in the cold air, the silent communion between two beings in the winter woods. As consciousness slowly claimed him, he took note of the hush that settled over the cabin. The snowfall continued in a steady drift against the windows, and the wind had lessened to a low murmur, as though resting from the night's exertions. Inside, the stove's embers still glowed, a sign he had banked the fire well before bed.

He sat up, stretched his stiff arms, and listened for any hint of wildlife scurrying around outside. Nothing but the soft exhalation of the wind. Slipping off his bunk, he crossed the floor to stir the coals and add fresh pieces of firewood—small sticks first, then larger splits—to coax the stove back into a roar. In minutes, heat radiated through the cabin's single main room, bringing new life to the chilly morning.

His first real act of the day was to shake his canister of coffee grounds, measuring a few scoops into his percolator, then topping it with water from the jug near the stove. The tin percolator went onto the heat, and as George worked around the cabin, he kept an ear out for that familiar *bloop-bloop* of boiling water cycling through coffee grounds. That sound, along with the pine-scented warmth of the stove, always reminded him how precious small comforts were. For a man who chose to live alone in the deep north, a hot cup of coffee was akin to a daily blessing.

He arranged his workspace with quiet efficiency—rolling up the blankets on his bunk, straightening the slender bookshelf, and setting last night's dishes into a small basin for washing. Today, he planned to stay closer to home, given the accumulating snow outside. The ice on the lake still wasn't thick enough to bear his weight safely once he ventured beyond the shoreline, so he'd save the possibility of ice fishing for another time. Besides, his food supply remained robust. Yesterday's trek had satisfied his desire for exploration, and he had enough chores indoors to keep him busy until midday.

He poured his first mug of coffee, inhaling its earthy fragrance, and sipped it at the table. From this vantage point, he gazed through the frost-framed window. Flakes drifted gently across the hazy expanse of the lake. Occasionally, a gust from the north would send a swirl of powder ghosting over the frozen shallows, creating pale ribbons across the surface. The forest beyond stood silent, evergreens stoic under their snowy burden. George realized he'd never tire of this view: a living painting, changing shape with every breath of wind or shift in temperature.

As the cabin grew warmer, he shed his topmost layer—a thick wool sweater—and switched it for a lighter flannel shirt. Then he pulled his journal from a nearby shelf. Before he wrote, he paused to reread the entry from the previous day, which described in detail the bull Moose encounter. His sketches were rough, more outlines than portraits, but they captured enough for him to recall the awe of that moment. Now, pen in hand, he added:

January 4th: Snow continues, calmer winds today. Fire keeps the cabin warm. Feeling grateful for the quiet morning after yesterday's excitement.

Moose sighting still fresh in my mind. Planning to stay in, read, tie flies, and keep the stove well fed.

Setting the journal aside, he unrolled a small portion of newspaper on the table and reached for his fly-tying materials. Winter in the north woods provided a natural stretch of time for this craft; the countless hours indoors became an opportunity to restock his tackle for warmer months. With the vice secured, he selected a hook and a spool of fine black thread. His vision was to create something that might tempt a finicky trout come spring—a variation on a classic nymph pattern with a bit of sparkle along the abdomen. In a methodical rhythm, he wrapped the thread around the hook, added tiny gold wire ribbing, and affixed a small tuft of marabou at the tail. Now and then, he glanced over at the stove to make sure the flames were steady. The cabin felt especially cozy when the wind wasn't rattling the shutters.

After completing a few flies, George stood to stretch and walk around the cabin. He looked at the old camera on his workbench. While it was an outdated model, it still functioned well enough to capture the essence of these snowy landscapes. He wondered if the day's subdued light might lend itself to some moody, monochromatic shots. But a quick peek through the window indicated the visibility was low. Fine snow, almost like a mist, blanketed the lake and the forest beyond, blurring lines and shapes. Perhaps he'd venture out in the afternoon if the snowfall eased.

Instead, he turned his attention to the corner of the cabin where he kept his oil paints, brushes, and a small folding easel. In summertime, plein air painting was one of his great joys, but occasionally, on a calm winter day, he liked to set up near the window and capture the stark scenery from the warmth indoors. He gently touched the bristles of a favored brush, remembering the day he'd last used it: a brilliant fall afternoon when the aspens were ablaze in gold, and the lake reflected the sky's deep blue. The painting he'd made that day, propped now against the wall, still brought him satisfaction. Winter's palette was subtler—shades of gray, white, and muted brown—yet no less majestic.

He considered setting up his easel to attempt a quick winter landscape, but first, breakfast beckoned. He laid out a skillet on the stovetop, sliced a thick piece of bacon from a slab he'd cured himself, and let it sizzle in the heat. The bacon's aroma filled the cabin, blending with the faint sweetness of the birch logs crackling in the stove. When the meat was nearly done, he spooned in some leftover beans from the previous day, letting them warm through. A simple meal, but satisfying. He ate slowly, listening to the gentle ping of snow tapping against the window.

Outside, the overcast sky made it difficult to discern the precise hour. The winter sun, low on the horizon even at midday, offered little in the way of clarity or warmth. George didn't mind; he found comfort in the extended twilight of these northern winters. They afforded him hours for reading, writing, and introspection that life in a busier place might not allow. After washing his dishes in a metal basin with heated water, he finally set up his easel by the window.

He tacked a small canvas board onto his easel, squeezed out dabs of oil paint—titanium white, Payne's gray, burnt umber, ultramarine blue—and began sketching the outline of the lake's far shore. The line of pines, nearly swallowed by mist and blowing snow, became a gentle smudge across the canvas. He used the edge of a flat brush to scrape at the shapes, capturing the essence rather than the details. This kind of painting felt like a dance between the real and the abstract. With winter light so diffuse, sharp detail was elusive; everything seemed soft, blurred, and secretive.

As he worked, the swirl of the brush transported him to a calm mental place. The rest of the world faded, replaced by the whispering hush of snow. The only interruption came when he needed to warm his fingers near the stove. Now and then, he sipped what remained of his coffee, now lukewarm, or paused to note a sudden gust that rattled the glass. The painting progressed slowly, a faint reflection of the subdued landscape outside.

Midway through, an unexpected motion caught his eye. He glanced out the window to see a single Fox trotting along the frozen edge of the lake, its red-orange fur a startling contrast against the white expanse. The Fox moved with that typical quick, light gait, pausing every so often to cock its ears and listen for potential prey beneath the snow. George held his breath, enthralled, wondering if he should reach for his camera. But sometimes, simply observing was enough—no technology interposed, no frantic scramble for a shot. He savored the scene. After a moment, the Fox continued on, disappearing into the tree line. With a faint smile, George added a sliver of orange to his canvas, a subtle nod to the spirit of the woods.

By early afternoon, the painting stood mostly finished—a monochromatic winter scene with just a whisper of color. He decided to let it dry near the stove, propping it up on a narrow shelf away from direct heat to prevent cracking. Art was not his primary pursuit, but each piece felt like a love letter to the land that had become his home.

Next, he took a moment to tidy his brushes, wiping off excess paint with rags and cleaning them gently in a small jar of solvent. Once done, he let them air-dry. The cabin smelled faintly of linseed oil, woodsmoke, and the bacon he had fried earlier—a combination that reminded George there were many forms of beauty in living simply and close to the earth.

After a glance outside revealed that the snowfall was finally easing, George seized the opportunity to step out for a short walk. He wanted to gather more birch bark for kindling—an essential fire starter in damp conditions—and perhaps test the lake ice near the shore again. Though he doubted it had grown thick enough to venture out far, he preferred to keep an eye on its progress.

Bundling up in his coat, gloves, and boots, he carefully opened the cabin door. The still air greeted him, cold and invigorating. Snow still floated down, but more sporadically, and the clouds above had lightened to a dull silver. He trudged through drifts that reached almost to his knees in places, grateful for the traction of his boots. As he circled around the cabin, he spotted the woodpile resting beneath its makeshift roof, a thin layer of new snow dusting the top. The stacked logs represented hours of previous labor—cutting, splitting, hauling. He had enough for this winter, and if it ever came close to running out, the forest stood ready to offer more as long as he harvested responsibly.

He continued onward, forging a path to a small copse of birch near the shore. Birch bark, with its papery layers, was highly flammable and invaluable for fire-starting. George peeled several strips from fallen branches, taking care not to injure any living trees. He placed the bark in a canvas pouch he wore slung across his shoulder. Meanwhile, he listened for signs of animal life. The forest felt subdued, as though the wildlife was taking refuge from the chill. Even the Chickadees, typically so vocal, only occasionally chirped from well-hidden perches.

Reaching the lakeside, he paused to gaze across its frosted expanse. The blanket of snow over the ice sparkled in what little sunlight pierced the clouds. He inched out only a foot or two, chisel in hand, and tested the surface. It felt firmer than the day before—maybe two and a half inches of ice near the shore—but still precarious for heavier travel. He tapped further out; the resulting sound was hollow, a cautionary note from the depths. With a small smile of acceptance, he withdrew. No sense rushing. This entire life was about patience, especially in winter.

Satisfied, he turned back toward his cabin, the soft crunch of his boots echoing in the still air. As he neared home, a sudden flurry picked up, swirling around him in a playful gust. He laughed, pulling his scarf tighter. Winter could be whimsical as often as it was harsh. Letting the wind guide him, he trudged the final steps to the porch. Once inside, he removed his gloves and exhaled a puff of steam that hung in the warm air of the cabin. The steady heat from the stove enveloped him, immediately loosening the tension in his shoulders.

He set the birch bark on a small hook near the fireplace where it could dry. Then he added another log to the stove. The day's light was waning again, though it was only mid-afternoon. He had discovered over many winters that the gray skies of January often made dusk arrive earlier than the clock suggested. This was a time he typically devoted to reading. After removing his coat and scarf, George selected a favorite volume from his bookshelf: an anthology of nature essays. He settled into his rocking chair near the fire, letting the dancing flames illuminate the yellowed pages. Outside, the wind rose and fell like the breath of some hibernating beast, a steady reminder of the world just beyond the cabin walls.

He read about naturalists who roamed places far beyond his forest—explorers in desert canyons, tropical jungles, and arctic tundras. The variety of Earth's landscapes fascinated him. At times, he felt a tinge of wanderlust, a craving to witness other corners of the world. But then the wind would sigh against the eaves, or he'd catch the comforting crackle of a log in the stove, and he'd remember that he had already found the place that fed his soul. There was no urgent need to chase experiences across the globe when each day here was so rich with small wonders.

Several pages in, he came across a passage describing the beauty of solitude in nature. The essayist wrote of how quiet spaces allow the mind to settle, enabling a person to notice life's intricate details—a leaf's vein, a snowflake's unique geometry, the sound of water flowing under ice. George found his thoughts drifting to the Fox, the Moose, the call of distant Wolves. He felt a kinship with these creatures, each one carving out its existence in a landscape shaped by challenging winters. He made a mental note to write down a quote from the essay later, perhaps in his journal, as it resonated with his own experiences.

When the light grew too dim for reading, he lit a lantern on the table, adjusting the flame until it cast a warm, steady glow. He set the book aside, then rummaged in a small chest for his old deck of playing cards. While not a gambler, he sometimes played a game of solitaire in the evenings—a habit that helped him unwind. The deck was well-worn, corners softened by years of shuffling. He laid out the cards in seven piles, letting his mind focus on the rhythmic flipping, the small triumphs of building suits, and the mild frustration of a losing layout.

Sometime later, he noticed that the wind had grown stronger again, whistling through the cracks in the cabin's logs. He stood and walked to the window, peering outside. The snowfall had resumed, heavier than before, and dusk had fully settled. The swirling flakes obscured much of the view, leaving only the faint outline of a few nearby pines. He suddenly felt grateful that he had stocked the woodpile earlier and had no pressing reason to venture out until morning. Winter nights like these could be both beautiful and unforgiving.

With that in mind, he decided to prepare a hearty stew that would provide warmth and comfort. He filled a pot with water, diced some potatoes and carrots he'd stored in a root cellar behind the cabin, and added dried herbs from his little spice box. For protein, he cut bits of venison jerky he had cured last autumn. The aroma soon filled the cabin, blending with the ever-present scent of smoke and pine. While the stew simmered, George took a moment to stand at his small window, sipping the last of his afternoon coffee (reheated over the stove) and watching the darkening world outside. The swirl of snow in the lantern-lit gloom was mesmerizing.

By the time the stew was ready, night had fallen completely. George ate slowly, savoring each spoonful of thick broth and tender vegetables. The wind hissed against the window, and the snowfall rattled the shutters. This was the winter he knew so well—a winter of extremes, from silent mornings to fierce nights. Yet he found solace in knowing that within these log walls, he was sheltered, warm, and nourished. The stew's steam curled upward, fogging his beard and reminding him of the fragile line between comfort and the harsh elements outside.

After washing his bowl and spoon, he took another log from the stack by the stove, carefully feeding the fire. Sparks danced up the flue, lighting the interior of the stove for a moment like tiny, swirling fireflies. George then settled into his rocking chair again, letting the stew warm him from within. He reached for his journal, wanting to capture the day's quiet progress:

January 4th, Evening. The second day of steady snow—gentle at first, but now a heavier fall under strong winds. Spent most of the day indoors. Painted a winter scene from the window. Spotted a Fox crossing the ice. Haven't heard Wolves tonight, but I can sense the forest is alive under this blanket of snow. A stew for dinner, hearty and rich. The cabin is warm, and for that, I'm thankful.

He paused, tapping the pen against the page. Something in him wanted to reflect on the deeper gratitude he felt—how each day in the woods offered a kind of meditation on life's essential elements: warmth, sustenance, awareness. He continued:

I'm reminded that no matter how fierce the storm outside, there's a peace in knowing one's place in the land. Solitude can be daunting, but it also clarifies what matters most—self-reliance, respect for nature, and a sense of quiet wonder.

Satisfied, he closed the journal. Then he turned to a small wooden box near the hearth. Within it lay an assortment of letters he had received over the years—rare correspondence from old friends, a couple of holiday cards, and a note from a relative who once visited him in warmer months. George seldom received mail, and the small post office in the nearest town rarely had anything waiting for him. Most folks knew he preferred a solitary life, though some worried he might get lonely. He appreciated their care, but in truth, he only occasionally felt a touch of solitude, quickly replaced by gratitude for the freedom to live as he did.

He thumbed through the letters, recalling the times they arrived. A holiday note from a cousin in the city mentioned parties, bright lights, and bustling streets. George respected that way of life— it just wasn't his own. Another letter, from a fishing buddy named Walter who lived a few hours south, recalled a summer trip they'd taken to a chain of lakes known for bass and walleye. George smiled at the memory of drifting in a canoe, the steady rhythm of casting, the excitement of a fish taking the lure. Perhaps, he thought, he might invite Walter up once the ice had melted in spring. It would be good to share a quiet paddle or two.

Outside, the wind howled anew, shaking the shutters so vigorously that George decided he should secure them better. He slipped on his coat, gloves, and hat, then stepped onto the small porch, lantern in hand. A blast of frigid air stung his face. Snow whipped in ghostly curls, stinging his cheeks and swirling past the lantern light. Quickly, he fastened an extra latch to the shutters and hammered a wedge between the shutter and the frame to keep it from rattling. Satisfied, he turned back to the cabin door. The short excursion into the storm reminded him of just how wild nights could get up here.

Once back inside, he stomped the snow off his boots and hung his coat. The warmth of the cabin embraced him immediately, and he felt his cheeks tingle as they thawed. He set the lantern aside and closed the door against the dark night, turning the iron latch until it clicked. For a brief moment, he stood in the center of the cabin, absorbing the stillness. The glow of the stove, the lantern's gentle circle of light, and the swirling storm outside formed a sanctuary of sorts.

He took a final moment to check on the painting he had completed earlier. The oils were still tacky, but they were drying well enough near the stove. The scene depicted a hushed, gray expanse with faint silhouettes of pines. Hardly a vibrant piece, but it carried the feeling of winter—a portrait of the very day he had lived.

Before bed, George decided to read another chapter from his anthology. He was partial to an essay describing the ancient forests of the Pacific Northwest—places he had never visited but could imagine, thanks to the vivid descriptions. The writer spoke of towering firs cloaked in emerald moss, of endless drizzle, and the haunting call of ravens echoing through mist-shrouded valleys. Despite the differences between that world and his own, George found parallels in the universal language of nature: the hush of old-growth timber, the interplay of life and decay on the forest floor, and the primal rhythms that governed all living creatures. By the time he finished the essay, he felt both comforted and inspired, reminded that his corner of the woods was but one facet of a vast, interconnected tapestry.

With a sigh of contentment, he placed the book on the table and stood up. The cabin was still, save for the crackling of the fire and the distant moan of wind outside. George latched the stove door to bank the fire for the night. A healthy bed of coals would keep him warm until morning; a quick feeding at dawn would bring the flames roaring back. He checked that the front door was bolted—like the shutters, it needed to be secure. All seemed well.

Finally, he crossed to his bunk, dragging out a heavy wool blanket to layer atop the existing covers. He knew tonight's storm might drive the temperature down, and though his stove was reliable, he preferred to sleep swaddled in warmth. He turned down the lantern flame until only a soft glow remained, just enough to navigate the cabin without stumbling into furniture. Then, nestled in his bunk, he let the events of the day wash over him.

The silence of the forest was not empty; it vibrated with unseen life—small mammals scurrying beneath the snow, owls perched in trees, and perhaps a lone Wolf prowling the shoreline for a meal. George felt his eyelids grow heavy. In the subdued flicker of dying lamplight, he whispered a small thanks for the day's simple gifts: the Fox sighting, the comfort of a hot stew, and the quiet fulfillment that came from painting a winter scene as it unfolded outside his window.

As his mind hovered at the threshold of sleep, the wind's wail through the trees rose momentarily, a lonely yet oddly comforting sound. He pulled the wool blanket higher, burying his chin into its soft folds. The routine of these winter days—chopping wood, painting, reading, writing, and listening to the hush of snowfall—gave him a profound sense of belonging. Each day, he felt more rooted in the land, more in tune with the forces that shaped it. Sleep came gently, like snowflakes settling onto a drifting landscape, and George drifted off with a final image in his mind: the warm glow of firelight dancing on the cabin walls, reminding him he was home.

By morning, he would wake to a cabin cooled but still welcoming, the stove ready for a fresh log or two. He would open the door to whatever new gifts winter had left in the night—fresh drifts, new tracks, and maybe the faint imprint of some nocturnal wanderer. But for now, he rested in the knowledge that even in the fiercest storm, the firelight's glow and the sturdy walls he'd built stood firm against the cold. The silent reflection of winter days offered him a deeper awareness of life's simple truths—each breath, each spark, and each small beauty in the snow.

3

ICE FISHING

A day or two after the storm that rattled his shutters, George awoke to a new kind of quiet—the kind that descends once the wind ceases and the world outside lies still under a white, pristine blanket. It was mid-January now, and his third week of deep winter in the woods. He opened his eyes to find the cabin surprisingly warm, thanks to the coals he'd banked overnight. As he rose from the bunk, he felt a hum of excitement. Today was the day he would test the ice in earnest and, if all seemed secure, begin his first serious ice fishing excursion of the season.

He dressed in layers: heavy wool socks, thick thermal underwear, a flannel shirt, and his warmest sweater. Over that, he donned his fleece-lined pants and a sturdy coat to block out the chill. He tugged on his boots and stepped to the woodstove, which glowed with the remnants of last night's fire. Carefully, he added a split of maple, then shut the stove door, listening to the new log hiss and crackle.

The early light outside seemed pale against the frosted windows, but George could see that the snowfall had stopped. He paused to admire the gentle glow of dawn illuminating the snowdrifts. Before anything else, he needed coffee. He measured grounds into his percolator—a routine that felt like second nature—and poured water from the jug. The hiss of fresh coffee on the stove brought a small smile to his face. While he waited, he wandered to the window to peer out at the lake, just visible through the slender trunks of birch. The ice looked as if it stretched in unbroken whiteness as far as his eye could see.

In the few days since his last checks, the temperature had plummeted, dipping below zero most nights. If luck was with him, the ice might now be four or five inches thick at least a dozen yards from shore—enough to safely hold him and his gear. The anticipation sparkled in his chest. Ice fishing carried its own charm: the crisp air, the hush of the frozen lake, the thrill of reeling up a fish through a circular portal in the ice.

He poured himself a mug of coffee, added a splash of milk, and gathered a quick breakfast of biscuits from the day before. He toasted them lightly in a skillet, letting the edges crisp, and topped each half with a smear of butter. Fuel for the hours ahead. He ate at his little table, savoring each bite, while mentally reviewing his ice fishing checklist. Auger. Sled. Tip-ups. Rod and reel with a short jigging rod. A bucket to carry his catch, if fortune smiled on him. Extra clothes and an insulated thermos of hot tea. He'd bring a small folding chair, too, though he often ended up standing near his fishing holes, lost in contemplation.

After breakfast, he finished off the last of the coffee and washed up quickly. With methodical precision, he began collecting the items he'd need. He stowed the hand auger, a chisel for testing ice thickness, and a few tip-ups in a small wooden sled—one he'd fashioned himself from sturdy pine slats. Next came a battered thermos he filled with steaming black tea, plus a small tin of biscuits, cheese, and jerky. He strapped his short rod and reel to the side of the sled along with an extra spool of line.

Before stepping out, he wrapped a thick scarf around his gray beard and donned his fur-lined hat with ear flaps that tied snugly beneath his chin. He grabbed his mittens and double-checked the stove. Placing one final log inside, he muttered, "That should keep the place warm enough to come back to." With that, he opened the cabin door onto a landscape hushed by fresh snowfall.

The wind was minimal, the air cold enough to burn his nostrils. He drew in a deep breath, exhaling a white plume. The path he'd shoveled around the cabin was half-filled with drifted snow, but he trudged through it easily with the sled in tow. The clouds overhead were thin and high, tinted with pale pink by the rising sun. The sky promised a day of cold clarity, the kind that set the pines shimmering.

Reaching the shoreline, he paused to do what he called his "ice reconnaissance." Using the chisel, he poked and prodded the lake's edge. It felt solid. He stepped out a few feet and gave the ice a firm jab. It held without cracking. Encouraged, he continued, each footstep followed by a deliberate test with the chisel. After traveling a safe distance— perhaps fifteen yards—he knelt down to drill a small test hole. The auger's blade bit into the ice with a satisfying screech, spiraling out shards of frosty slush. Once he broke through, he used a small metal measuring rod to check the thickness: just over five inches. That was good enough for him and his modest load. He'd still keep an eye out for any changes or pressure ridges, but for now, he felt confident.

He trudged onward, scanning for a likely fishing spot. In summer, he knew this part of the lake for Lake Trout—especially near a drop-off roughly twenty yards from shore, where the depth plummeted from ten to thirty feet. While the exact location was harder to pinpoint on a snow-covered lake, he used the shoreline's shape to guide him. Once he thought he was close, he dropped the sled's rope and began drilling his first real fishing hole. The work was strenuous, but the excitement of what lay beneath the ice propelled him.

The auger broke through with a final groan, and George scooped out the slurry of ice shavings. Clear water welled up, reflecting the bright sky overhead. He placed the auger aside, took out his short jigging rod, and threaded it with fresh line, deciding on a small jigging spoon tipped with a piece of salted minnow. Once the lure was attached, he lowered it into the hole. The lake water, impossibly cold, sent up a faint mist where it met the air. George propped a small stool behind him and prepared to wait.

But he didn't wait long. Within minutes, he felt a subtle *tap-tap* on the line. His heartbeat quickened. Slowly, carefully, he lifted the rod tip, setting the hook with a gentle flick of his wrist. The rod bent; a fish was on. It fought in short, sharp bursts, typical of Lake Trout, thrashing in the frigid water. George reeled in steadily. The hole was just wide enough to guide the trout's head up, and with a final tug, he pulled it onto the ice. It was a modest fish, maybe fourteen inches, gleaming silver-gray with light spots. A grin spread beneath his beard. "Well, that's a good start," he murmured.

He took a moment to admire his first catch of the season, then quickly dispatched it and placed it in the sled's bucket. The cold air would keep it fresh until he got home. Pulling the fish made him all the more eager to set up a few tip-ups. Tip-ups would allow multiple lines in the water, each rigged with a minnow or a jig for Lake Trout or Walleye. He selected three tip-ups from the sled, spaced them in a rough triangle around his main hole, and set each line to drop just off the bottom. His father had taught him many years ago: "Fish cruise just above the lakebed in cold weather, especially trout and walleye." Whether that held true for every lake, George couldn't say, but it often proved right in this one.

Soon, everything was rigged. He scanned the lake's emptiness. Snow spread in a broad, flat expanse, dotted only by the occasional small ridge or drift. The forest circled the shore like a silent audience. He couldn't see any neighbors or even footprints other than his own. Though remote, the scene felt comforting, not lonely. This was his world—where he belonged.

Time slipped by in the easy manner typical of good fishing days. George jigged his rod lightly every so often, imparting a flutter to the spoon. He sipped occasionally from his thermos, relishing the warmth that blossomed down his throat. He listened for movement in the woods, for the slightest hint of a breeze. He checked his tip-ups methodically, scanning for the telltale orange flag that would pop up when a fish took the bait.

Eventually, a flag sprang upright on the tip-up to his left, snapping him from his reverie. He nearly spilled his tea as he scrambled over the ice. The spool below the flag was spinning, line peeling off quickly. George knelt, carefully lifted the mechanism, and pulled the line taught. When he felt the weight on the other end, he gave a quick tug, setting the hook. This fish was bigger. It dove under the ice, shaking its head. George fought steadily, letting line slip between his mittens when the fish made a run, then gently guiding it toward the hole. This battle lasted a good two or three minutes, each moment thrilling in its uncertainty—would the fish throw the hook, or would he manage to coax it onto the ice?

Finally, he glimpsed a flash of silver in the watery darkness. He maneuvered the fish's head up through the hole, and a thick-bodied Lake Trout came thrashing onto the surface, water spraying in arcs. This one was closer to twenty inches, with vivid white spots and a graceful, tapering shape. "Well now," George said, panting lightly, "you'll make a fine meal." His breath steamed in the cold. He dispatched the trout and took a moment to admire its colors, feeling a surge of gratitude. A fish like this could feed him for multiple meals, or he could set some aside for tomorrow. There was no need to catch more than he'd eat soon.

He cradled the fish and placed it in the sled beside the smaller one. A sense of triumph and contentment washed over him. This was the reward for braving the elements and respecting the rhythms of the lake. He had plenty of chores back at the cabin, but at that moment, none seemed as urgent as soaking in the stillness. He decided to remain for a few more hours.

Sitting on his stool with his jigging rod, George felt a shift in the weather. The sky, once pale blue, had begun to gather clouds again. Not storm clouds, just a heavy winter blanket that turned the afternoon light into a diffuse glow. A mild breeze stirred, blowing across the lake and collecting snow in tiny swirling eddies. In the distance, he caught a flicker of movement along the treeline—a pair of Coyotes, perhaps, trotting single-file. He could just make out their lean shapes as they wove between pines, likely scanning the shoreline for rodents or winter-weakened prey. For a moment, he stopped fishing to watch them, heart full of wonder. They didn't seem to notice him or if they did, they paid him no mind.

With the afternoon half gone, George checked his tip-ups again. No new bites. The jigging rod remained quiet as well, so he decided it might be time for a quick lunch. He rummaged in his sled for the tin that held biscuits, cheese, and jerky. While he ate, the cold pressed in, nipping at his exposed cheeks. He pulled his scarf higher and shifted his stool so his back was to the slight breeze. The quiet was immense, broken only by the occasional pop of ice shifting beneath him—sub-surface cracks that resonated like distant thunder. He'd grown used to these sounds; they no longer startled him, merely reminded him of the living body of water beneath his feet.

By the time he finished lunch, the afternoon light was fading, and the temperature began to drop sharply. He decided it was wise to reel in, collect his tip-ups, and head back. His day on the ice had been successful enough: two Lake Trout, plus the deep satisfaction that came from time spent in nature's silent realm. He packed everything, sliding the fish carefully into the bucket. With a final glance at the shimmering hole in the ice, he turned toward shore. Dragging the sled behind him, he retraced his steps, carefully avoiding any area that looked thin or cracked. It took only ten minutes before he was back on solid land.

The sky dimmed as he trudged home, though it was still mid-afternoon. In January, darkness fell early. He left a single set of footprints in the fresh snow, which soon would be partially obscured by the drifting wind. That notion always comforted him: how the land covered signs of human presence so quickly, returning to its pristine state.

Upon reaching the cabin, he stomped the clinging snow from his boots on the porch and set the fish bucket aside. The cabin door stuck slightly from the cold, but he gave it a firm push and stepped into the welcome heat. The stove still burned, though he needed to feed it more logs. Before dealing with anything else, he removed his gloves and hat, and he gently massaged warmth back into his chilled fingers. The transition from the biting cold to the cabin's warmth felt luxurious.

His next task: cleaning the fish. He kept a designated corner on the porch for such work, a small table where he could slice and rinse without fuss. Though the cold air nipped at him, he wanted to keep any mess out of the living space. With a sharp knife, he carefully gutted the smaller fish first, disposing of the entrails in a steel bucket he'd later bury in the snow a ways from the cabin. Then he moved to the larger trout. Its flesh was firm and pinkish, a sign of a healthy fish. "This'll make for a fine dinner," he said quietly. Even alone, he enjoyed speaking his gratitude. He filleted the larger fish, setting aside one fillet for the evening and salting the other to preserve for another meal.

After rinsing the table and his knife with water from a jug he stored outside—kept liquid by insulation—he wiped everything dry, then returned indoors. His cheeks burned from the chill, so he paused by the stove to thaw out fully. The logs he had added crackled and popped merrily, sending orange sparks up the chimney. George felt the day's exertion in his shoulders, a pleasant fatigue that accompanied any good catch or day of labor.

He decided to cook the fish right away. From a small cupboard, he retrieved a cast-iron skillet and some of the herbs he'd dried last autumn—thyme, bay, and a sprinkling of pepper. He placed the skillet on the stovetop to heat while he patted the fillet dry and rubbed it with salt. A piece of butter from his recent trip to town would give the fish a rich, savory flavor. Within minutes, the cabin filled with the warm scent of sizzling trout, the butter browning at the edges. He heard the oil sizzle, and soon the fish took on a golden hue.

As it cooked, he prepared a simple side dish of potatoes and carrots he still had in his root cellar. He diced them up, boiled them in a small pot, and then mashed them with a bit of butter and salt. Between that and the fish, it felt like a feast. When he finally sat down to eat at his wooden table, the sun had fully descended, leaving only a bluish twilight beyond the windows. He doused the lantern on his table to conserve fuel, relying instead on the flicker of the stove's firelight. Shadows danced across the log walls, creating an intimate, cozy glow.

His first bite of trout was delicate and flaky, infused with the subtle tang of fresh butter and the bright taste of herbs. With each forkful, he closed his eyes in brief appreciation. Days like this reminded him of the cycles that sustained him: the lake, the fish, the forest. He never took them for granted, never felt he was owed anything by nature.

Every success—be it a catch, a harvest, or even an animal sighting—felt like a gift.

After dinner, he washed the dishes in a basin of heated water. The routine movements brought him a sense of calm. Steam rose in gentle curls as he scrubbed the skillet. When it was clean, he dried it carefully and placed it back on the shelf. He'd learned long ago to keep gear in good shape—a neglected skillet or dull knife could complicate a simple life in the woods.

He then moved to his writing desk, a small surface beneath a lamp near the window. The storm shutters remained open tonight, the sky outside dotted with a few distant stars. He lit the lamp, adjusted the wick until it cast a steady glow, and opened his journal to a fresh page. The day's events poured out in a neat script:

January 7th: First true ice fishing trip of the season. The lake's ice measured around five inches. Caught two Lake Trout—one small, one quite sizable. The larger fillet made an excellent dinner. Also spotted a pair of Coyotes near the treeline. Quiet day, minimal wind. Thankful for a safe outing and the abundance the lake provides.

He spent a few moments embellishing his notes with a small sketch of a tip-up, recalling the moment the flag popped up. The memory made him smile. Then he tried to capture the shape of the Lake Trout, adding details to indicate its spotted sides. Though his drawings were simple, they helped him preserve the essence of each day's highlights.

Leaning back, he let the pen rest. The stove's heat radiated across his back, lulling him into a comfortable drowsiness. He considered reading for a while, perhaps a few more essays on wilderness travel or a chapter from a novel about explorers in a far-off land. But exhaustion from a day spent in the cold air settled over him like a warm blanket. Instead, he stood and carefully closed his journal, placing it atop the growing stack of filled notebooks. Each page, each entry, was a record of his life here, marking time by the rhythms of nature.

Outside, the wind had picked up again, rattling the branches of the nearest spruce. A faint rustling of snow drifted past the window. George approached the glass and peered out. The lake was no longer visible in the darkness, but he knew it was out there—silent, frozen, guarding secrets beneath the ice. On especially calm nights, the shifting of the lake's ice would resound in deep groans or popping sounds, like distant fireworks. He wondered if he might hear them tonight.

He took a moment to sip some water and stoke the fire before bed. As flames danced higher, he briefly thought of the fish he'd set aside—salted and stored in a sealed container. That would make an excellent lunch or dinner the next day. An image of tomorrow began forming in his mind: Maybe he'd take a shorter fishing excursion, or maybe he'd do some chores around the cabin. He also considered trying a different section of the lake soon, one known for Walleye. But that could wait. There was no sense in rushing anything out here.

When he felt satisfied that the cabin's warmth would last a few hours, he readied himself for bed. He slipped out of his heavy clothes, dressing in a thick flannel shirt and woolen sleep pants, then nestled into his bunk beneath a pile of blankets. The wind teased the corners of the cabin, but it lacked the force of the previous storms. Tonight felt calmer, a gentle hush settling over the woods. He pictured the coyotes loping through the snow, the fish resting at the bottom of the lake, and the silent flight of an owl scanning the moonlit forest for a midnight meal.

Before drifting off, George mulled over the day's sense of fulfillment. Winter life could be harsh, but it also offered these moments of honest work and quiet bounty. He felt a surge of gratitude for his own resilience, for the skill set he'd honed over the years to not just survive but truly thrive in the wilderness. There was a humility in it, too—recognizing that nature was always in control, and that he was merely a guest. Even as he caught fish from the lake, he tried to remain mindful of the balance required to keep these waters healthy. He took only what he needed, left behind no more than footprints in the snow. In return, the land gave him sustenance and a sense of profound belonging.

His bunk felt especially welcoming tonight, the layers of wool and down insulating him from the frigid air outside. The last sparks from the stove flickered across the cabin, the shadows dancing gently against the log walls. In that subdued light, George's eyelids grew heavy. He allowed his breathing to slow, the day's images forming a dreamy tapestry in his mind—the swirl of snow on the ice, the tug of a fish on the line, the afternoon hush as he waited for a flag to snap up.

Sleep overtook him in the pleasant knowledge that tomorrow promised its own small adventures, whether that meant another trip onto the ice, a trek through the snowy woods, or a quiet day of painting and reading by the stove. For now, the darkness cradled him in a peaceful lullaby, and the cold night beyond the cabin walls seemed far away. Ice fishing, with its quiet, contemplative moments and bursts of excitement, had given him one of the sweetest days of winter he could recall.

Outside, the wind sighed across the frozen lake, stirring the powdery snow into faint ghosts. The cabin stood firm, a warm island in the midst of the deep north. George slept soundly, lulled by the knowledge that he had spent the day in harmony with the season's rhythm—a man content in the winter wilderness, sustained by its gifts, respectful of its power, and eager to greet the next sunrise on the ice.

4

FIRST SIGNS OF SPRING

George awoke to find the world outside his cabin cast in a peculiar half-light, as though winter and spring were fighting for dominion over the day. The edges of his windows were still crusted with frost, but past that fragile barrier he could see a subtle melting taking place—the bank of snow that had been piled against the cabin wall since January was beginning to slump, forming jagged ledges that dripped with water. It wasn't quite warm yet, but there was a gentleness to the air, a slight softness that hinted winter was loosening its grip.

Stoking the stove, George took careful note of the temperature inside the cabin. He still needed a robust morning fire, that much was sure, but he could also sense the difference in the way the chill receded once the flames danced through the stove's glass pane. As he boiled a pot of coffee, he watched watery sunlight poke through the thinning clouds. The light carried a fresh hue—not the stark white brightness of midwinter, but something milder, almost golden. He listened for changes in the forest. Normally, deep winter brought a hush, punctuated by the occasional crack of ice or the lonely call of a raven. Today, however, there was a faint patter, as if small creatures were stirring in the undergrowth.

Over the past few days, George had watched the lake's ice go from solid to slushy around the shoreline. He had ventured out one final time with his chisel to test its thickness two afternoons prior, only to discover that while the center still held a decent sheet of ice, the edges were now precarious. Stepping onto the lake felt more like pressing down on a wet sponge than standing on firm ice. That alone told him the transition was underway. His ice-fishing gear was stowed for the season. The tip-ups, jigging rods, and sled would wait until the next winter arrived. For now, he focused on the promise of open water and the kinds of adventures spring would bring.

He poured a steaming mug of coffee, sat at his small wooden table, and looked over the notes he'd scrawled in his journal the previous evening. Sparse entries for the past week mostly described the slow retreat of winter: the snow depth shrinking day by day, the lengthening of daylight, the first glimpses of bare ground near tree bases where the dark bark absorbed the sun's rays. Most thrilling were the signs of wildlife reawakening. George had heard the flutter of returning birdlife at dawn—among them, a small flock of finches that sang brightly from the high branches of a pine. He'd even caught a glimpse of a plump Robin, though that might have been his imagination wanting to see the iconic harbinger of spring. Sometimes a few overwintered in certain microclimates, but if the Robins were truly back, the season's shift was near at hand.

Once he finished his coffee, George decided he'd spend the morning walking the perimeter of the lake to see how far the thaw had advanced. He could think of no better way to greet early spring than to observe its quiet progress firsthand. He dressed in layers, aware that the morning temperatures still hovered around freezing, but that the midday sun—if it peeked out—would warm things considerably. His heavy winter coat would likely be too much, so he settled on a lined jacket and a light scarf. He checked his boots to make sure they were still watertight; nothing spoiled a spring walk faster than wet feet in half-frozen slush.

Stepping out onto the porch, he felt a stirring deep in his chest, an eagerness that recalled the first day of school from his youth, full of possibility. The snow on his porch steps was soft, collapsing under his boots rather than squeaking as it had in the colder months. Water droplets glistened on the cabin's eaves. He paused to brush a few from his beard, which was already catching random snowmelt dripping from the roof. Across the clearing, the pines stood tall but less burdened by the thick mounds of snow that had draped their branches for so many weeks. Small clumps still clung here or there, but the shape of each limb was more defined. It seemed the whole forest was shaking itself free of winter's overcoat.

He started his walk along the lake's edge, weaving between the trunk of a birch and a large cedar that framed a small path. The snow in this area was patchy, revealing pools of slushy water around the tree bases. Each step was a careful negotiation; if he moved too quickly, his foot might plunge into a hidden puddle. But the mild challenge didn't bother him—he wore boots meant for precisely these uncertain conditions, and the small 'snap' of ice giving way beneath him was only a reminder that winter's grip was not absolute.

Reaching an outcrop of large rocks, he climbed up carefully. From that vantage point, he could see the entire northern half of the lake. The scene was both familiar and strange, as though the lake was in the process of shedding a layer of its skin. Large sections were still covered in milky-white ice, while closer to shore, the ice was dark and honeycombed, flecked with puddles of water where the sun had melted it from above. George noticed a cluster of Mallards swimming in a narrow channel of open water near the creek inlet. He felt a small surge of joy at the sight of those green-headed drakes bobbing on the surface—one of the earliest signs that migrating waterfowl were returning.

As he climbed down the rocks and continued along the shore, he spotted more evidence of life. A Squirrel scampered across a patch of exposed pine needles, pausing to nibble on something. A pair of Chipmunks skittered in and out of a small hole near a fallen log. Even the air smelled different—a wet, earthy scent that came from layers of decomposing leaves finally thawing after months of being locked in ice.

Making his way around a gentle bend, George suddenly heard a sharp crack, followed by splashing. He froze, heart pounding, until he realized it was not the sound of someone or something falling through the ice, but rather a Beaver gnawing a branch near the water's edge. The Beaver slapped its tail against a slushy patch of ice, creating the splash. George crouched behind a nearby bush, peering around it to get a better look. Indeed, there it was—a robust Beaver with sleek, dark fur, working diligently at stripping bark from a fresh limb. The ring of teeth marks on the branch confirmed how busy this creature had been. The Beaver's presence was another sure sign that the lake's inhabitants were gearing up for the warmer seasons—repairing lodges, gathering materials, and establishing territory.

He quietly retreated, not wanting to disturb the industrious creature. Moments like this reminded him of how intimately connected each part of the ecosystem was. Soon, the streams feeding into the lake would be rushing with snowmelt, raising water levels and giving the Beavers ample opportunity to expand or shore up their dams. With each passing day, the watery realm of spring would broaden, and new life would fill these woods.

By the time he returned to the cabin, the sun had risen high enough to warm his back, and he found himself loosening his scarf. He paused near his woodpile, noting how much the logs had settled as the snow that once encased them melted away. He decided he wouldn't need to chop more firewood today; the stockpile was ample, and the nights, though still cold, were growing milder. For a moment, he gazed at the path leading to the small root cellar. Much of the snow around it was gone, revealing soggy ground. The thought of the first wild greens that would soon start poking through the forest floor made him smile. Nettles, ramps, fiddleheads—these would come with the true spring, providing fresh tastes after a winter of more monotonous fare.

Stepping inside, he peeled off his jacket and set it over a chair to dry. The warmth of the cabin felt luxurious compared to the damp chill outside, though it was no longer the biting cold it had been mere weeks ago. He brewed another pot of coffee—something about the changing season gave him an extra craving for that cozy comfort. While the water heated, he rummaged in his cupboards for the last of his winter root vegetables. He had a few carrots and potatoes remaining, a testament to his careful planning back in autumn. Soon, he would start craving fresher produce, but for now, these staples would have to suffice. He decided to make a simple soup for lunch, letting the vegetables simmer slowly while he recorded his observations from the morning in his journal.

Sitting at his small table, he wrote:

March 2nd: The ice is retreating along the shoreline. Saw Mallards, a Beaver, and signs of squirrels and chipmunks. Snow on the ground is thinning—dripping everywhere. Smells like spring in the air, even if the nights are still cold. The forest is waking up.

He paused, running his hand over his beard, which had grown even bushier through the winter. He thought back to previous springs spent here— how each year carried its own nuances. Some springs came late, snow clinging stubbornly into April. Others arrived in a rush, with violent spring rains that erased winter in days. This year seemed somewhere in between, a gradual, steady thaw that gave him time to appreciate each subtle transition.

A gentle steam rose from the pot on the stove. He stirred the soup, adding salt and some of the dried herbs he had left. Thyme, a bit of oregano. A savory aroma soon filled the cabin, mingling with the faint smell of woodsmoke. As the soup simmered, George picked up a well-worn field guide to birds. He flipped through pages, refreshing his memory of the species most likely to return in early spring. Red-winged Blackbirds, Blue-winged Teals, maybe even the boisterous Canada Geese if they chose this route. Perhaps within a week or two, he'd see a pair gliding overhead, honking in that familiar call that heralded the changing season.

After his lunch, he washed the dishes, then decided to spend the afternoon focusing on one of his favorite hobbies he'd mostly set aside during the coldest months: plein air painting. Oh, he had dabbled a bit in winter scenes from inside the cabin, but there was something different about setting up his easel in the open air. The day's mildness suggested it might be time to do exactly that, even if he had to pick his spot carefully to avoid sinking in slush. He gathered his portable easel, a small canvas, brushes, and a light palette of oils. Then he rummaged for an old blanket to stand on or fold under his feet. Spring might be coming, but the ground was still cold and wet.

Outside, the midday sun was bright enough to cast a soft glare on the remaining snow. George shielded his eyes with one hand while scanning for a good vantage point. He found a small rise near a cluster of birch trees, where a portion of the lake was visible, and the dripping ice at the shoreline formed intriguing patterns. Setting up his easel, he planted the legs firmly in the snow and tested their stability. Satisfied, he laid the folded blanket on the ground so he could stand in one spot without soaking through his boots.

He began by sketching the general shapes in charcoal: the faint silhouette of the far shore, the ragged edge of retreating ice, and the reflection in the pools of open water. Then he squeezed out a limited palette of colors onto his wooden tray—white, ultramarine blue, burnt umber, yellow ochre, and a hint of green. Capturing early spring was more challenging than painting full summer or deep winter. The scene was subtle—browns and grays, slushy whites, half-dead grasses peeking through the snow, and subdued reflections on the water. He started with broad strokes, blending the browns and blues to form the distant shoreline. Next, he dabbed careful touches of white and gray to mimic the partially melted ice. Despite the modest palette, he found the painting absorbing, a meditation on the interplay of water, ice, and land.

As he worked, the forest around him seemed quietly abuzz with life. He heard an occasional rustle of wings—a small bird flitting from branch to branch. The drip-drip-drip of melting snow served as a gentle percussive track. Now and then, the groaning of lake ice carried across the water, echoing in the still air. George felt an almost childlike wonder. It was as though each drip of melting snow was a promise—spring was not just a date on the calendar but a living, breathing transition. Every living thing sensed it, and the forest was poised to burst with renewed energy.

He painted until the sun dipped lower, the temperature cooling enough that a chill crept into his fingers. Carefully, he packed away his supplies and placed the wet canvas on a small shelf in the cabin's entryway where it could dry without smudging. Stepping back inside, he stripped off his damp boots. His toes tingled from the time spent standing on partially frozen ground, so he warmed them by the stove, rotating his ankles to coax circulation back. Hunger gnawed at him, and he realized the day had passed more quickly than he'd expected. A hearty supper was in order.

That evening, George opted to cook the last piece of salt-preserved trout he had from his winter ice-fishing. He stewed it gently with onions and a bit of leftover soup broth, creating a sort of chowder. While it cooked, he thumbed through one of his nature diaries from years past, searching for references to the earliest spring sightings. He found an entry from a time when winter had broken quite early—mention of hearing frogs as soon as mid-March. Another year, not so long ago, it was late April before the ice was truly gone. Reflecting on these records reminded him that nature's rhythms, while cyclical, were not always predictable. Each year offered a distinct personality.

As the chowder simmered, the cabin filled with a comforting, savory scent. He ladled a portion into a deep bowl and sat near the stove, letting the fire's glow illuminate his meal. The flavors were rich and nostalgic, a taste of winter's bounty giving way to spring's new hopes. Afterward, he washed up, then decided to treat himself to a small glass of whiskey—a rare indulgence he savored in these transitional times. He took a seat in his rocking chair, swirling the liquid in a simple tin cup and sipping slowly. Outside, the day's last light faded, replaced by a dim silver in the west. The lake lay invisible in the darkness, though he could imagine the slush quietly shifting.

That night, before bed, he made one final entry in his journal:

The ice recedes inch by inch. Painted the shoreline today—amazing how many shades of gray and brown exist when you truly look. Mallards have returned. Could spring peepers be far behind? The air is full of possibility.

He closed the journal, feeling satisfied and a bit drowsy. With a final check of the stove, he banked the coals, leaving them to smolder until morning. Then he crawled under his blankets, the rustle of fabric reminding him of countless nights spent in this cabin—each season cycling through in its own time. Sleep came easily, filled with dreams of flowing water and green shoots.

The following days brought more unmistakable signs of spring. One morning, George awoke to the bright chatter of Chickadees near his window. The next, he spotted the first fresh blade of grass pushing up through a melted patch beside a rock warmed by sunlight. The changes occurred so rapidly he could almost see them happening in real time. Great patches of bare earth emerged around the pines, and small trickles of meltwater carved rivulets into the once-frozen ground, creating mini-canals that sparkled in the sun.

He decided to gather some new supplies for the shifting season, which meant a trip to the nearby town. In winter, he'd only ventured there a couple of times, mostly for essentials like flour, coffee, and butter. Now, with the roads clearing, the journey would be easier. He loaded his truck with empty containers for fresh provisions, making sure to pack a list of items he needed: seeds for the small garden bed he liked to tend when the ground thawed fully, extra lamp oil, and a few fixings to keep life cozy—maybe a new spool of strong thread for his rods, or a fresh notebook for journaling.

The drive into town was an education in spring's messy in-between stage. Potholes pitted the main road where thawing and refreezing had done their annual damage. Snowbanks along the shoulders were streaked with dirt, like old white rags that had seen better days. Yet the sky above was a brilliant blue, and the sunshine bathed everything in a gentle warmth. George navigated cautiously, mindful of ice patches in the shaded hollows. Occasionally, he'd see a flash of bright color—a cardinal darting across the road or the red of a barn newly revealed by melting drifts.

In town, the mood was buoyant. People seemed eager to emerge from winter's hibernation. Shopkeepers propped open doors to let in fresh air, and the general store had placed seed packets on prominent display near the entrance. The local café bustled with chatty locals sipping coffee, discussing the latest news: the roads, the thaw, the talk of migrating flocks spotted further south. George picked up his usual staples—coffee, flour, a block of butter—and treated himself to a small wedge of cheddar. He found some sturdy seed potatoes and onion sets, plus a few packets of carrot, bean, and lettuce seeds. Though it might be another month before the ground was truly ready, the mere act of purchasing seeds filled him with anticipation.

He stopped in at the hardware store to check out new lines for fishing reels. Chatting with the store owner, Carl, a longtime resident who called

George simply "the old mountain man," he learned that the chain of lakes further west was thawing fast. By April, Carl guessed, the trout streams there would be open and running strong. George considered a future trip—maybe he'd load up his canoe and do a portage once the water was safe to navigate. Just thinking about paddling among pines and budding willows put a spring in his step.

After a quick bite at the café—a welcome treat after winter's isolation—George headed back on the winding road. The sun was lower in the sky now, illuminating the landscape with a softer glow. He drove slowly, mindful of deer that might be emerging at dusk to feed on newly exposed vegetation. Sure enough, he spotted several at the edge of a field, cautiously nibbling the fresh shoots. One raised its head, big ears alert, but it didn't bolt. It seemed to sense that George meant no harm. Moments like this were a silent communion—man and animal sharing the land in parallel.

Upon returning to his cabin, he unloaded his haul. He placed the seeds in a cool, dry corner, anticipating the day he could sow them in the warming earth. The fresh groceries went into his simple pantry, and he gave himself a moment to enjoy the hush of home. The sun was setting in a blaze of pink and orange, reflecting off the patches of half-melted ice on the lake. Still no open water near his shoreline, but a large swath of dark water had formed in the middle, roiling gently where the warming winds had broken the ice. It wouldn't be long now before the entire lake was free of winter's hold.

That evening, as he set a kettle to boil, George felt the strong pull of possibility. Spring was not only a shift in temperature but a renewal of spirit. The forest animals would be more active; soon he might see a Black Bear stirring from its den, a Moose browsing on tender shoots, or the first new leaves popping from aspens. He thought of the painting he'd started and considered continuing it, capturing each stage of the thaw as days went by. But for now, he simply wanted to sit quietly, sipping tea, letting the moment settle in.

He pulled a chair to the cabin's window, looking out at the dusk. The pink sky had faded to a smoky lavender, and the lake surface glowed faintly in that final glow of evening. A single star appeared overhead. Through a gap in the trees, he saw a thin crescent moon. In the hush, he picked up the faint trickle of water beneath the ice—a sound like a quiet heartbeat of the land. Leaning back, he closed his eyes, allowing the rhythms of nature to wash over him. The sense of promise in the air was almost tangible.

Before bed, he wrote in his journal:

Spring in her early form. Roads are muddy, snow receding, birds returning. Mallards on the lake, beaver busy at the shore, deer in the fields. Picked up seeds in town—looking forward to planting soon. Painted a thawing scene by the birch trees. Cabin life feels lighter, each day longer and warmer. Winter is letting go, but gently.

He concluded with a small sketch of the rising moon, capturing the curve of the crescent and the hint of pines beneath it. Then, with a tired but contented sigh, he banked the coals in his stove. The cabin would grow chilly by dawn, but not too much. Each day saw less need for the roaring fires that were a staple of midwinter. As he sank into his bunk, the blankets felt inviting rather than absolutely necessary for survival. He drifted off to the gentle drip of melting snow, lulled by the knowledge that spring was coming in earnest— softly and steadily, bringing new life, fresh colors, and a world of small wonders awaiting his discovery.

That night, a gentle rain began to fall, tapping softly on the cabin roof. In the weeks prior, such precipitation would have arrived as sleet or snow.

But now it came as a mild shower, pattering across the shingles, trailing down the eaves in sparkling ribbons. George slept soundly through it, though he occasionally stirred to half-wakefulness at the unfamiliar noise, a reminder that the season had shifted. By the time dawn broke, the world outside glistened with raindrops, the old snow further eroded by the mild onslaught. He stepped onto his porch, greeted by a fresh earthy smell so different from winter's crispness. A thin layer of ice had melted completely from the edge of the porch, revealing the sturdy planks for the first time in months.

He took a slow breath, letting gratitude swell in his chest. Spring wasn't fully realized yet—there could still be a stray snowstorm or a biting frost. But it was undeniably on its way, carrying light and life across the north woods. Soon, the forest would be alive with new shoots, budding leaves, and the rustle of creatures old and young. The lake would break free, and his canoe would glide once more on open water. And George, content in his log cabin at the edge of it all, would greet each new sign of spring with the same gentle reverence: a quiet smile, a line written in his journal, and a heart wide open to the unfolding beauty of the season.

5

WILDLIFE ENCOUNTERS

The first night George heard the frogs singing in the wetland near his cabin, he knew spring had truly arrived. The chiming chorus echoed through the mild evening air, each trill and croak a testament to the season's new life. He listened from his front porch, a steaming mug of tea warming his hands, and let the amphibian choir wash over him. The last of the ice on the lake had finally melted a few days earlier, leaving a free expanse of shimmering water behind. In a single week, the woods had transformed from slush and half-snowdrifts into carpets of browns, greens, and delicate buds waiting to unfold.

The days were growing noticeably longer now, sunshine lingering well past supper. George woke each morning to a cacophony of birdsong: Robins, Chickadees, the occasional Blue Jay, and even a pair of Canada Geese that had claimed the small peninsula across from his cabin. He could hear their honks echo across the lake as he made his morning coffee. Sometimes, he'd stand by the window, cup in hand, and watch the geese waddle along the grassy edge, flapping their wings at any interloping ducks that ventured too close. The air smelled different—damp and loamy, like the forest floor had exhaled after a long hibernation.

Since the warmth had taken hold, George found himself busier than he'd been all winter. There were tasks to see to that simply couldn't be done with three feet of snow on the ground. He cleared the narrow garden patch behind his cabin, raking away dead leaves and bits of mulch that had sat frozen for months. The soil beneath was still dark and cold, but turning it revealed shy earthworms and a rich, earthy scent that promised fertile ground for the seeds he'd purchased in town. A week or two more, he reckoned, and he might be able to plant onions, carrots, and beans without worrying about a heavy frost rolling in overnight.

His canoe, unused since late autumn, had been propped against the side of the cabin all winter, covered in a tarp. With the weather warming, he decided to inspect it for damage. The hull was a bit dusty, the paint dull from months of exposure to icy winds, but it seemed structurally sound. He carefully wiped away the grime, running his hand along the edges, checking for cracks or warping in the wooden gunwales. Satisfied that the canoe was still seaworthy, he left it resting on saw-horses to let the sun and gentle breezes finish drying out any remaining moisture.

Although chores filled much of his time, George also felt the renewed pull to explore. He planned to take his camera on a springtime walk, hoping to capture the first blooms of trout lilies and trilliums that often appeared around this time of year. But more than anything, he was eager to see what the local wildlife was up to. After months of trudging through waist-deep snow—or sometimes gliding atop it on snowshoes—he could now wander the woods with lighter gear, feeling the muddy earth yield beneath his boots.

On a mild morning with a soft breeze, George set out on foot, his camera slung over his shoulder, a small rucksack containing a water bottle, a map, and some snacks strapped across his back. Dressed in a light flannel shirt and weatherproof pants, he felt almost unburdened after the heavy layers of winter. The sun had barely climbed above the tallest pines when he stepped into the woods, following a faint trail that skirted the lake's eastern shore before winding inland.

Almost immediately, he noticed changes. The undergrowth that had been flattened by snow was springing back to life. Small ferns curled their bright green fronds upward, and mosses glimmered on fallen logs. He could still see pockets of old snow in shaded dells, where the sun rarely touched, but they were shrinking fast, forming miniature streams that trickled toward the lake. The air brimmed with birdsong. Every so often, a flash of color—blue, red, yellow—announced a different species perched among the budding branches.

George soon saw fresh tracks in the damp earth. First, the delicate hoofprints of Deer, heading toward the lake for a morning drink. Then something bigger: elongated marks that suggested Moose. The prints pressed deep into the mud, each larger than the span of George's hand. He knelt, tracing the outline with a finger. Judging by how sharp the edges were, these tracks might be only an hour old. Heart quickening, George scanned the surrounding pines and birches, half expecting to see the Moose browsing in the distance.

Continuing along the path, he soon smelled something pungent—damp fur, old leaf litter turned over. He suspected that a Moose or possibly a Black Bear had recently moved through. Black Bears were known to stir from hibernation around this time, hungry and keen to replenish lost weight.

Though usually shy and non-confrontational, a bear stumbling upon an easy meal—like an unprotected garbage can or leftover winter berries—could be unpredictable. George made a mental note to remain alert.

A short while later, as he climbed a slight rise, he heard branches snapping to his left. Soft footfalls, heavier than a deer's. He eased to a stop behind a cedar trunk and peered through the foliage. Sure enough, there at the edge of a clearing stood a Moose—a large cow with thick, dark fur. She was stripping bark from a young sapling, her massive head bobbing as she chewed. George felt a rush of awe. Even after years living in these woods, sightings like this still stirred a childlike excitement. He raised his camera slowly, focusing on the Moose's profile. The click of the shutter was barely audible, but the Moose's large ears swiveled in response. For a tense moment, she paused her chewing, scanning the trees. George held his breath, heart pounding. She must have decided he was no threat, because she soon resumed her meal.

He managed a few more shots before leaving her in peace, treading softly away so as not to disturb her further. The new season had clearly brought renewed feeding opportunities for the Moose, with tender shoots and bark exposed by the melting snow. George made a note in his mind to add these observations to his journal later. Encounters like this were the highlights of his day, sometimes even his entire week.

The next morning, George was in his cabin tidying up after breakfast when a sudden commotion outside drew his attention. He heard a scratching noise, accompanied by the hollow thump of something pawing at wood. He froze, listening carefully. Bears could be quite curious when they awakened, especially if they picked up a food scent. Cautiously, he stepped toward the window that overlooked the side of the cabin where his canoe and extra supplies were stored.

Peering outside, he almost gasped: a Black Bear, still somewhat lean from winter's fast, was snuffling around the stacked cords of firewood. The Bear pressed its broad muzzle against the lower logs, as if searching for a hidden morsel. Perhaps a mouse nest was lodged inside, or the Bear smelled leftover fish scraps that George had once rinsed away nearby. For a moment, George merely watched, enthralled by the Bear's size and the thick black fur that caught the morning sun. Then he remembered that a Bear so close to his doorstep was not exactly safe for either of them—wild animals got in trouble quickly if they grew comfortable around human dwellings.

George eased open the window just a crack and spoke in a firm voice, "Hey there, buddy. No food for you here. Best move on." He clapped his hands loudly, the sound echoing off the cabin walls. The Bear stiffened, lifting its head. Its small brown eyes fixed on the noise, ears twitching. With a huff, it turned, lumbering off into the pines with a slow, rolling gait. George's heart hammered as he watched it disappear. Bears generally avoided conflict, but a hungry one could be persistent. He made a mental note to secure any potential attractants—like the fish cleaning table on his porch or the sealed container where he disposed of scraps. He also decided to take an extra trip to check his root cellar door. If it wasn't latched tightly, a Bear might pry it open.

Once the Bear was gone, George exhaled, half relieved and half exhilarated. He'd grown accustomed to living among creatures that city folk rarely encountered. Still, he would never lose respect for their power and unpredictability. He reminded himself to remain vigilant in these transitional weeks. The Bear's reappearance around his cabin was a sure sign of spring's progress—though he hoped future visits would be less direct. After all, a Bear rummaging too close could become bolder if it found food, and that was trouble for them both.

As spring advanced, the forest teemed with activity. George continued his daily wanders, sometimes carrying his camera, other times simply observing. He found fresh sets of fox tracks zigzagging across patches of moist ground. Once, just after sunset, he glimpsed a red Fox slinking along the lakeshore, its bushy tail trailing behind like a banner. The Fox froze when it saw him, ears perked, muzzle quivering. George remained still, letting the Fox decide its next move. After a few moments, it darted away, leaving only the memory of bright eyes and a flash of orange against the twilight.

In another instance, he heard yipping from a distant ridge—a small pack of Coyotes vocalizing at dusk. He had grown to love that eerie, high-pitched harmony, though it sometimes set him on edge late at night. Coyotes were opportunists, skilled at surviving in varied habitats. He wondered if they would cross paths more often now that the snow had melted. He recalled the winter tracks he'd seen near the cabin. But these thoughts didn't trouble him too much. Coexistence was simply part of life out here. As long as he kept his provisions secure, there was little reason for concern.

Near the lake's inlet, the local Beavers had been busy as well. Their dam, battered by winter storms, now showed signs of fresh repair—new branches laid skillfully across the old framework, coated in mud and leaves. George sometimes stood at the water's edge with his binoculars at dusk, watching them float logs toward the dam with single-minded determination. He admired their craftsmanship; each branch was positioned with intention, water lapping gently around the construction. The pond behind the dam, once locked in ice, now shimmered with reflected pine trees.

One sunny afternoon, George set up his folding chair on a small knoll near that inlet, determined to catch the Beavers on camera in better light. He waited an hour or more, munching on crackers, letting the gentle breeze lull him into a state of calm. Finally, a ripple spread across the water. A sleek, dark head emerged, beady eyes scanning the shoreline. George lifted the camera, zooming in. Snap—he captured the Beaver's head, water droplets shimmering on its fur. It swam closer to the dam, paddling with that trademark wide tail, then dove under the surface with a splash. George grinned, reviewing the shot on his camera's display. He'd caught the moment perfectly, the Beaver's profile outlined against the ripples. Another precious piece of spring documented.

Of course, the forest's vegetation also erupted in new growth. Everywhere George looked, plants stretched eager shoots toward the sky. Trout lilies with their mottled leaves dotted the damp forest floor, while trilliums unfurled three-petaled blooms of white or maroon. Late one morning, he ventured deeper into a grove of maples and birches, hoping to find early ramps—those pungent wild leeks that made for wonderful soups and sautés. A keen eye helped him spot the bright green leaves poking up through the leaf litter. He harvested a modest handful, enough to flavor a couple of meals, leaving the rest to repopulate. That evening, he sautéed the ramps with butter and a sprinkling of salt, mixing them into a simple pasta dish. The taste was sharp yet fresh, an echo of the wild land just outside his door.

As the undergrowth thickened, George also kept watch for fiddleheads—young, curled fern shoots that were a delicacy in many parts of the north. Sure enough, in a damp area by a trickling stream, he found a cluster of tightly coiled fronds. He carefully snipped a few, mindful not to overharvest any single patch, and brought them home. A quick blanching and a light toss with garlic turned them into a fresh, crunchy side dish. After a winter of tinned beans and root vegetables, these flavors felt almost extravagant. He imagined the forest teeming with energy just beneath the surface, urging every plant to push skyward in the weeks to come.

One drizzly afternoon, George decided to hike the same path where he'd seen the Moose earlier, hoping to see how the terrain had changed. The sky was overcast, the forest quiet except for dripping water and the occasional rush of wind in the treetops. He wore a light rain jacket, camera tucked under his arm to keep it dry. The earthy smell of wet pine needles and soggy leaves enveloped him as he walked.

He had just begun to ascend a slight incline when he heard it—a soft grunt, low and rumbling, from somewhere ahead. He froze, stepping carefully behind the broad trunk of a spruce. Another grunt sounded, this time closer. Peering around, he spotted movement among the birches: a massive bull Moose. George's breath caught in his throat. He hadn't seen a bull Moose in months. This one was thinning out from the winter, and his antlers were in velvet—new growth that would fully harden in the coming months. The Moose stood in a patch of emerging greenery, tearing at fresh shoots with heavy lips.

A wave of reverence swept through George. The bull was an imposing sight, even in the gentle rainfall. Its wet fur glistened, droplets sliding off broad shoulders. Steam rose faintly from its flanks. George raised his camera, careful not to make sudden motions. He snapped a single photo, the shutter sound masked by the raindrops pattering on leaves. The bull Moose jerked its head up, ears swiveling. For a tense moment, man and beast locked eyes. George's heart hammered. A bull Moose, even without fully developed antlers, could be dangerous if it felt cornered or spooked. He kept still, letting the Moose decide what to do next.

The bull exhaled loudly, nostrils flaring, then returned to chewing. Feeling he'd pressed his luck, George quietly retreated, stepping backward until the Moose was out of sight. Only then did he turn and continue along another route. He felt almost giddy, the adrenaline coursing through him. Times like these reaffirmed his gratitude for living in a place where wildlife roamed free, sharing the woods and the water. The photograph he'd taken, if it turned out well, would be a treasure—a moment of raw nature caught in the hush of spring rain.

Though the days were warmer, nights could still carry a chill. George typically lit a small fire in the woodstove at dusk, just enough to chase away the dampness. By that time, he was often tired from hours spent wandering, foraging, or tending to cabin chores. He'd ladle a bowl of soup or stew—sometimes spiced with the ramps he'd gathered—and settle in near the warm hearth.

With his big gray beard and lined face, he looked every bit the picture of a solitary woodsman. Yet he felt anything but lonely. The animals, the forest, the rhythm of the lake—they formed a tapestry of quiet companionship. He kept a stack of nature books at arm's reach, as well as the newest pages of his journal. When the mood struck, he'd flip through photographs on his camera, deleting the blurry ones and marveling at the clear shots that captured some fleeting moment of wildlife in action: the Beaver carrying a branch, the Fox's curious stare, the Moose in velvet.

At times, George painted. Now that the temperatures were milder, he could keep the door cracked for fresh air, letting the sound of frogs and distant birdcalls seep into the cabin. One evening, he embarked on a detailed watercolor of a single trillium bloom. The bloom's crisp white petals contrasted against deep green leaves, and he aimed to capture the subtle shadows and delicate veins. The process was meditative, each brushstroke an act of devotion to spring's fragile beauty.

Occasionally, he indulged in reading or rereading older journal entries from previous springs. He found a certain satisfaction in comparing notes—dates when the ice broke, sightings of particular animals, or the earliest wildflowers he'd encountered. Over the years, he'd come to recognize patterns: the Black Bears often showed up by mid-April, the frogs started singing once nights stayed reliably above freezing, and the Moose migrated from deeper woods to shoreline stands of young growth. All of it felt like a grand cycle, a symphony that repeated with seasonal variations, year after year. And he, George, was privileged to stand in the midst of it, observing, partaking, and finding contentment in the simplest revelations.

One morning, just as the sun was cresting the horizon, George stepped outside to gather a few logs for the stove. The sky blushed pink and orange, painting the lake's surface with shifting colors. As he lifted an armful of split birch, he heard yips and barks echo from across the clearing. This was different from the distant calls he sometimes heard at night—it sounded close, urgent. Setting the firewood down, he crept around the corner of the cabin.

Down by the edge of the lake, near a rocky patch where the water lapped against still-dark waters, stood three Coyotes. Their coats looked mottled in the early light—gray, tan, and rusty brown. They seemed focused on something near the waterline, noses low. Perhaps a fish carcass or a washed-up treat from the thaw. One coyote snapped at the shallows, while another wagged its tail in excitement.

George stood still, heart thudding, observing from a safe distance. He'd rarely seen them so clearly in daylight. They were smaller than wolves, but still elegantly built—long snouts, bushy tails, and keen ears. The trio circled the edge of the lake, yipping softly, then one lifted its head, catching George's scent or movement. Immediately, it grew still. The others followed suit, all ears swiveling, bodies tensed. For a moment, man and coyotes regarded each other under the brightening sky.

He felt no fear—only a rush of wonder. Coyotes were elusive creatures, wary of human presence. Often, he only knew they were nearby from tracks or distant howls. This up-close glimpse in the dawn light felt like a gift. Knowing they might spook if he moved too abruptly, George remained rooted, letting them decide what to do. After a few seconds, one coyote barked sharply, and the trio darted away along the lakeshore, their bodies lithe and quiet. Within moments, they vanished into the band of poplars that ringed the lake's north side.

Releasing a breath, George continued to the woodpile and gathered the logs. His pulse fluttered at the memory of those bright eyes. Encounters like that reminded him of the careful balance between humans and the wild—how quickly the forest gave and then reclaimed the moment. He stacked the logs by the stove, feeling a wave of gratitude wash over him. The day was still fresh, and already he'd been given something remarkable.

Later that same day, the sunshine felt warm enough for George to try sowing the first seeds in his small garden. The ground, though moist, was no longer frigid. He hoed the soil, breaking it into a soft, crumbly texture. The smell of fresh earth filled his nostrils. Removing a packet of onion sets and another of carrots, he planted them in neat rows, labeling each with a small wooden stake. For the beans, he decided to wait another week or so—he'd read the weather patterns enough to sense a final frost might still sneak in, and beans hated the cold.

As he worked, he could hear a chorus of bird calls from nearby pines. The soil clung to his hands in dark clumps, a stark reminder of how different the world was from just a month earlier, when everything lay entombed in ice and snow. Basking in the sunshine, he paused to remove his flannel shirt, working in just a light undershirt. The air felt glorious on his skin.

When the seeds were in place, he watered them gently with a small can, collecting water from the lake's edge in a bucket. The lake water was still cool to the touch, but in the midday sun, it felt less harsh than it had a few weeks ago. He imagined the seeds nestled in the warm soil, poised to sprout into green shoots that would feed him in the months ahead. This cyclical process—planting, tending, harvesting—was part of what made his life in the woods so grounded. No matter how advanced technology became elsewhere, here, he relied on age-old rhythms and simple manual labor.

That night, George decided to turn in early. The events of the past few weeks—seeing a Moose, scaring off a Bear, hearing Coyotes at dawn, and gathering ramps from the forest floor—had filled him with a contented exhaustion. Sitting by the fireplace, he sipped on a cup of chamomile tea and flipped open his journal. He'd been diligently recording each wildlife encounter, each sign of nature's renewal.

He wrote:

April 16th: Spring in full swing. Garden is partially planted—onions and carrots, beans soon. Encountered a bull Moose with velvet antlers, a humbling sight. A Black Bear near the woodpile reminded me to stay vigilant. Coyotes seen at dawn by the shore—three of them, lively and bold. Beavers are repairing their dam, Fox spotted on the far side of the property. The forest hums with life.

He paused, tapping his pen against the blank space. In the soft glow of the lantern, he reflected on what spring truly meant for him. It wasn't just a shift in temperature or a change in the color of the leaves. It was a season of awakening—of animals rediscovering their territories, of plants pushing toward the light, of the lake returning to its fluid identity. And for him, it was a reminder that time marches on with or without human interference. He felt a sense of profound gratitude for being allowed to witness it so closely.

The land teaches patience and renewal. Each year, I watch winter fade into memory as new buds burst forth. It never fails to humble me.

Satisfied, he closed the journal. The cabin was warm, the stove crackling quietly. Outside, the frogs had begun their nocturnal chorus again, joined by the faint rustle of a night breeze stirring budding branches. George blew out the lantern and stood in the darkness, feeling the steady heartbeat of the woods around him.

Moments like this confirmed that even though he lived alone, he was never truly by himself. The forest, the lake, and all the creatures formed a living community. He was merely one part of a vast web of life, each node vibrating with energy. Slipping under his blankets, he allowed the gentle, living lullaby to guide him into sleep—frog calls, distant coyote howls, the hush of wind across water. And in the morning, the cycle would continue: new growth, new encounters, and the same quiet wonder that reminded him each day why he chose to live his life in the woods.

6

A TRIP TO TOWN

The first rays of sun filtered through the pines as George stepped out onto his porch, a list of provisions tucked into the pocket of his flannel shirt. The morning air was clear and brisk—pleasantly cool after the mild warmth of the previous days. Though winter's snows had fully retreated from the clearing around his cabin, the ground remained soft and damp, a testament to the recent weeks of thaw and rain. The sweet smell of turned earth filled the air, mingling with hints of pine sap and the faint musk of last night's rain on the forest floor.

He paused on the porch steps, inhaling deeply, then descended to check the narrow dirt driveway that wound from his cabin through the woods. After months of being mostly snowbound, traveling into town required caution—muddy patches, deep ruts, and a few remaining potholes might conspire to make the journey trickier than usual. But, from what he could see, the track looked passable. The day had come for his first real trip to town since winter had broken.

He walked around the cabin to where his old pickup truck waited beneath a makeshift shelter—a simple roof of corrugated metal propped on tall wooden posts. He'd bought the truck secondhand a decade ago, and its blue paint had long since faded. Speckles of rust lined the edges, giving it the look of a true workhorse, worn but steadfast. He patted the hood affectionately, as though greeting an old friend.

"Let's see if you'll start without a fight," he said with a quiet chuckle, remembering the times he'd coaxed the reluctant engine to life in subzero temperatures. Now, with the air warming each day, he expected fewer protests from the old girl. He climbed into the driver's seat, turned the key, and listened as the engine sputtered once, twice, then roared into a steady rumble. A triumphant smile creased his bearded face.

He let the truck idle while he took stock of his supply list. The long winter had whittled down his stores. He still had enough flour to make bread for another week or two, but coffee was running low, and he'd been out of butter for days. Milk, too, was on the list, along with some new fishing line if he could find it at the hardware store. He'd also promised himself one small indulgence: a few library books, if the local branch happened to have anything interesting.

Pleased that the truck was in working order, he stepped out to retrieve his traveling gear. Along with his usual duffel containing empty jars for restocking dried goods, he brought a small cooler. If the town grocer had something special—like fresh produce or local eggs—he wanted to keep them chilled for the drive home. Once everything was in place, he double-checked that his cabin was secure, shutters latched, and stove banked so no embers posed a risk. Though the stove was not lit this morning, he always ensured there was no stray spark that might cause trouble in his absence.

As he climbed back into the truck, a pair of Chickadees fluttered across the clearing, their morning chatter echoing among the pines. He took a last look at the cabin, feeling a gentle tug of anticipation. He didn't visit town often—usually just a few times each season—so the outing felt like an event, equal parts practical errand and social excursion.

Shifting into gear, he guided the truck along the narrow path, the tires sloshing through a shallow puddle left by recent rainfall. The forest soon swallowed the cabin from sight. As he drove, the morning sun streamed through breaks in the canopy, casting long stripes of light across the road. The earthy smells of spring enveloped him, stirring memories of past journeys: trips where he'd braved muddy roads, pitched tires in deep ruts, or had to clear fallen branches from the route. Today, however, the drive felt calm and straightforward— a sign that nature, while still awakening, was offering a gentler transition into the new season.

Roughly a mile in, the dirt path joined the main gravel road leading toward town. Here, the going was smoother, though still dotted with puddles. George steered carefully, mindful of any hidden washouts. Past experience had taught him that beneath an innocent-looking surface might lurk a deep, tire-sucking trench. He rolled down the window an inch, letting in fresh air laced with the scent of cedar and damp leaves.

After another few miles, the gravel road gave way to a paved highway. Only then did George relax his grip on the wheel. He glanced at the truck's dashboard clock—still functioning despite being decades old—and noted it wasn't yet eight in the morning. Good. He'd make it to town before midday, allowing ample time for errands and maybe a leisurely lunch at the café.

He passed a few isolated homesteads, smoke curling from stone chimneys. At one point, he spied a wild Turkey hen and her brood darting across the pavement, causing him to tap the brakes. The fuzzy chicks scurried after their mother, all of them vanishing into the roadside brush. The scene brought a smile to his face—springtime was truly a season of new life. The miles continued to roll by, the forest lining each side of the road in dense waves of spruce, pine, and newly budding hardwoods.

By late morning, George rounded a final bend and caught sight of the small town. A simple wooden sign proclaimed its name—Kincaid Falls— though the "Falls" part was more historical than literal. The nearest significant waterfall was miles away, but the name had stuck since the days of early logging camps. The main street was modest, just a handful of businesses and a smattering of houses branching off into side roads. A single traffic light hung above the intersection near the heart of town, blinking yellow in a languid pattern. He rolled through, nodding to a passing car whose driver lifted a hand in greeting.

George brought his truck to a stop outside the general store, a low brick building with a wide wooden porch. The facade boasted old-fashioned signs for milk, bread, flour, and sundries. Colorful planters flanked the entrance, filled with pansies and marigolds that signaled the official start of the planting season. He noticed a few folks chatting on the porch—neighbors catching up on local gossip, no doubt. As he killed the engine and climbed out, the muffled chatter on the porch went momentarily quiet.

"Morning," he called, giving a polite wave. A couple of them nodded and smiled in return. An older man, wearing suspenders over a plaid shirt, offered a friendly greeting. "Well, if it isn't George. Haven't seen you in a coon's age! How's the old cabin holding up?"

George approached, feeling the slight awkwardness that always accompanied these interactions. He was a self-sufficient man, not used to small talk, but he appreciated the warmth in the question. "Holding up just fine, Burt," George answered. "Winter was a tough one, but it's giving way to spring now. How about you? This mud season treating you all right?"

Burt chuckled and shrugged. "Ah, you know how it is. Some days I think half my yard will end up stuck to my boots. But we'll manage. Good to see you out and about."

George returned the grin, made a bit more small talk, then excused himself. He stepped into the store, blinking as his eyes adjusted from the bright sun to the softer indoor lighting. Immediately, the cozy scent of spices, old wood floors, and burlap sacks enveloped him. Along the shelves, bags of flour and sugar were neatly stacked, alongside canned vegetables and other staples.

Behind the wooden counter stood Marlene, the store's longtime proprietor. She was a petite woman with short silver hair, her face etched by years of kind smiles and worry lines. She beamed at George's entrance. "Well, look who decided to stop in before summer! Good to see you, George."

He removed his hat, nodding politely. "Good morning, Marlene. Winter was a busy one—didn't make it to town as often as I'd planned. But I'm running low on supplies now, so here I am."

Marlene smiled, resting her hands on the counter. "You always do this at the perfect time. We just got a shipment of fresh butter in yesterday, plus a new batch of coffee beans from that roaster I was telling you about last fall. The fancy kind, you know, with a hint of chocolate or something."

George's eyebrows lifted with interest. Though he was a simple man, he had a soft spot for good coffee. "That so? Might have to splurge a little."

She nodded vigorously and began listing the other items newly in stock—fresh eggs from a local farm, jars of honey, and a selection of preserves that a nearby orchard put up every spring. George let her guide him through the aisles, picking out the staples first: a sturdy sack of flour, several pounds of coffee, a tub of butter, and, of course, a carton of milk. He also added a jar of local honey, remembering how it sweetened his tea in the colder months.

"I'll be sure to have the rest of my groceries shipped up here more often," George joked. "Or maybe I should just make a point of coming to see you more regularly."

Marlene chuckled. "You say that every time, but I know you cherish your quiet life in the woods. That's all right by me—just don't wait till you're scraping the bottom of the flour barrel to show up next time."

He grinned, gently rolling his eyes at his own predictability. "I'll try to come in sooner. But you know me, once I'm up there, I lose track of time."

Shaking her head in affectionate exasperation, she tallied up the goods, then carefully packed them into two sturdy paper bags. "Now, if you need anything else, just holler. And say hello to Linda at the café. She was asking about you last week, said she hadn't seen your beard around in ages."

That mention of Linda and the café reminded George that it had been a while since he'd treated himself to a hot meal cooked by someone else's hands. The memory of Linda's homemade pies nudged him toward a decision. "I might just do that," he said, hefting the grocery bags. "Thanks, Marlene. I'll pop these in the truck and swing by the café."

He bid her goodbye, stepping out onto the porch again. The sun was higher now, warming the wooden planks. A handful of people still lingered, chatting about local matters: the state of the roads, the fishing prospects in the early spring, the rumor of a new family moving into the old Johnson place. George nodded politely as he passed, loaded his groceries into the cooler in the truck bed, and then locked the tailgate.

The café, just a few doors down, was housed in a squat wooden building painted a cheery red. A small chalkboard sign out front proclaimed: *Today's Special: Meatloaf & Mashed Potatoes, Slice of Pie, and Coffee—$8.50.* The sign was adorned with a whimsical doodle of a smiling cow and a slice of pie. He couldn't help but smile. He remembered Linda's meatloaf from years past, served with gravy rich enough to warm any heart. Stepping inside, he was greeted by the comforting aroma of fresh coffee and sizzling onions.

"George!" a voice called from behind the counter. It was Linda, wearing her signature apron printed with tiny daisies. Her warm face lit up in a grin that reached her kind brown eyes. "It's been too long. Come on in, sit wherever you like."

The café was modest—just a few booths, a row of stools at the counter, and several small tables scattered about. A few customers were already eating, glancing up with mild curiosity at the newcomer. George opted for a booth by the window, setting his hat on the seat next to him. He felt a subtle relief to be off his feet after trekking around the store.

"You want the special?" Linda asked, already grabbing a mug to fill with coffee. She didn't wait for an answer. "It's the best deal in town, especially for a man who's been living off the land all winter."

George chuckled. "I'll trust your recommendation."

"Cream and sugar, as usual?"

He nodded. "Yes, please."

She placed the steaming mug on the table, her gaze flicking over his shoulder-length hair and bushy beard. "You look good, George. Taking care of yourself up there?"

"As much as I can," he replied, warming his hands on the mug. "But I was sure missing butter and milk. I've been rationing coffee for the last week, too, so this is a treat."

Linda frowned sympathetically. "Well, next time, drop by sooner. I'll pack you a care basket if you need one. We can't have you up there going without your morning brew." She flashed a wry smile, then headed to the kitchen to place his order. He sipped the coffee, savoring its robust flavor. While he brewed a decent cup himself, there was something about the café's pot—maybe the seasoning of well-used equipment, or the intangible benefit of communal air—that made it taste extra satisfying.

When Linda returned with the plate of meatloaf, mashed potatoes, and gravy, George's mouth watered at the sight. The portion was generous. Alongside the plate, she set a small bowl of green beans with slivered almonds. "Eat up," she said with a wink, moving off to help another patron.

George took his time, cutting into the tender meatloaf and relishing each bite. He gazed out the window while he ate. From this vantage point, he could see the main street, the general store across the way, and the day's gentle traffic of neighbors running errands or visiting. A pair of kids biked past, squealing with delight as they dodged puddles. A stray dog trotted lazily on the sidewalk, tail wagging at everyone who passed. The hum of everyday life in Kincaid Falls felt comforting, even if his own routine was more reclusive.

His gaze drifted to the chalkboard listing pies. He recalled Linda's homemade fruit pies—apple, berry, sometimes rhubarb if the season was right. Sure enough, a small note read: *Try our Fresh Rhubarb Pie!* He still had half a glass of water left, but his appetite stirred for something sweet.

Linda must have read his mind, because she sidled up with a notepad. "Room for pie?"

He gave a sheepish grin. "Wouldn't be a trip to the café without it, would it?"

"Rhubarb it is," she said, jotting down. "You want it warmed?"

"Please."

She bustled away, returning moments later with a slice of rhubarb pie. The flaky crust glistened with sugar, and tangy steam curled upward from the filling. George thanked her and dug in, the tartness of the rhubarb balanced by the sweet pastry. Every forkful was a reminder of simpler joys that city folks might never fully appreciate. The sense of community, the flavor of a dessert grown in local soil, the kindness of a longtime acquaintance—these small-town comforts meant more to him than any fancy meal in a distant urban restaurant.

He finished the slice slowly, pushing his plate aside with a satisfied sigh. Linda reappeared, refilling his coffee. "How's the cabin? Anything new?"

George thought of the wildlife encounters he'd had. He described seeing the Moose with velvet antlers, the Black Bear rummaging near his woodpile, and the Coyotes by the shore. Linda listened intently, occasionally letting out a low whistle or exclaiming in surprise. Other diners glanced over, perhaps eavesdropping on the conversation.

"You ought to write a book," Linda said when he finished. "People flock here for that sort of wilderness story."

George shook his head, a soft chuckle escaping him. "I write in my journal enough as it is. But I like keeping those moments mostly to myself. If I turn them into a spectacle, I'm not sure they'd feel the same."

Linda smiled in understanding. "Fair enough. You keep your secrets, old-timer." She gave his shoulder a friendly pat, then headed back behind the counter.

After settling the bill, George left a generous tip—he knew how much Linda valued each patron, especially during the quieter off-seasons. She tried to wave off his extra couple of dollars, but he insisted, a kind grin beneath his gray beard. "You can put it toward the next time I show up two months late for groceries," he teased.

She laughed. "Deal."

Stepping outside, George paused to admire the bright midday sun. The small amount of heat it radiated felt good on his shoulders. He walked the short distance to the town's hardware store, a squat building with red trim and wide glass windows. Inside, a bell chimed as he pushed open the door. Rows of tools, fishing gear, and household items lined the shelves. The faint smell of metal and motor oil reminded him of old workshop days.

He was greeted by Tim, the store owner, a lanky fellow with salt-and-pepper hair. "George! Haven't seen you in a while. Finally thawed out from your winter hideout?"

"Ha, pretty much," George said, scanning the aisles. "How's business?"

"Can't complain. Everyone's gearing up for spring repairs, yard work, you name it." Tim paused, tilting his head. "You after anything particular today?"

"I was hoping for some new fishing line. I used up most of mine this winter tying leaders for ice fishing. And I'd like to check if you have replacement bearings for a reel I might fix."

Tim led him to a display of tackle and reels. "We got a shipment last week of braided and monofilament lines. Take your pick. As for bearings, might have something that fits. Let's see..."

George studied the spools carefully, selecting a mid-range monofilament that matched the type he liked for trout and walleye. Tim rummaged in a small drawer behind the counter, pulling out a tiny bag of bearings. They talked fishing for a few minutes—reports of local hotspots, how the spring meltdown affected fish behavior, and which lures might be best. Tim mentioned that some folks had caught nice-sized walleye in a chain of lakes to the west, though the water remained a bit cold for topwater action.

"Well, if it stays mild, I might paddle my canoe out there in a week or two," George mused, tucking the spool of line under his arm. "We'll see if I can scare up a fish or two."

Tim smiled. "Let me know how you do, old man. And if you run into any trouble with that reel repair, come by and I'll lend you a hand."

George paid for his items, adding a small can of oil for reel maintenance. Thanking Tim, he stepped back into the sunlight. Next, he ambled over to the tiny library near the edge of town. The building was more cottage than grand institution— a single story, white clapboard walls, and a door painted a cheery turquoise. A wooden sign above read: *Kincaid Falls Public Library.*

Inside, the librarian, Mrs. Klinskey, sat behind a narrow desk, reading an oversized reference book. She was a bespectacled woman in her seventies, with curly gray hair pinned in a loose bun. She glanced up, recognized George, and broke into a warm smile. "Well, I don't see *you* very often. But I'm always glad when you do come by."

He returned her smile. "Sorry to burst in unannounced like this."

She waved a hand. "Don't be silly. Come in, come in. Let me guess—you'd like something nature-themed?"

George grinned. "I suppose that's my usual. But I'm open to suggestions."

She rose from her chair, beckoning him to follow. The library was compact, just a few aisles of books, a children's corner, and a reading nook with a worn armchair. Mrs. Klinskey led him to a small section labeled *Natural History & Outdoors.* She pointed out a new birding guide, fresh from the publisher. "This might be handy. It covers a lot of North American species with full-color photos. Also, there's a book about canoe routes through the upper lakes, if that suits you."

He took them both, flipping through the birding guide. The vibrant images caught his attention—Warblers, Woodpeckers, Loons, all in brilliant color. "This is perfect," he said softly, imagining the hours he'd spend comparing his real-world sightings to these pages.

Before heading back to the front desk, he also snagged a worn paperback novel from a shelf of local authors, curious to see how someone might fictionalize the area's wilderness. Mrs. Klinskey checked him out, stamping the due date on each book. "How long will you need them?" she asked gently, knowing his pattern.

"Probably a month," George replied. "I'll try to return them sooner, but you know how it goes."

She nodded. "No rush. We keep flexible due dates for folks who live off the grid. Just be sure you stay safe. If you need more time, call us—though I suspect you still don't have a phone."

He laughed. "Not likely. But if the weather's good, I'll come down in a few weeks. Thanks so much for these."

Tucking the books under his arm, George bade her farewell and stepped outside once more.

By early afternoon, he'd completed his errands. The once-empty truck now carried groceries, hardware, and borrowed books. He considered walking around town to see if there was any other business he might attend to—a quick check at the post office, perhaps—but decided it could wait. The gentle hum of conversation and the mild bustle of the day had filled him with just enough social energy; he felt the call of the woods urging him back. Besides, the cooler in the truck bed held perishables he needed to keep chilled.

He started the engine and pulled away from main street. The occasional wave from a passerby, the bobbing of the café sign in his rearview mirror—these familiar sights made him smile. Although he cherished his solitude, he also valued the safety net that came from being part of a small community, even on its outskirts. It was good to know people looked out for him, that a warm meal and friendly banter awaited whenever he ventured into town.

After merging onto the paved highway, he drove at a moderate pace, scanning for wildlife. The afternoon sun glinted off patches of standing water in the fields, and he saw a few Canada Geese pecking near a roadside pond. Soon, the highway gave way to the gravel road, and he navigated carefully around fresh ruts. By the time he reached the dirt track that led to his cabin, the forest canopy seemed to welcome him with rustling leaves and scattered beams of sunlight.

The final stretch was trickier—mud splashed around the tires, and he had to navigate around a fallen branch. Eventually, he spotted his cabin roof through the trees, just where he'd left it. He parked beside the woodpile and killed the engine. Silence enveloped him. A bird called from a nearby birch, and the breeze rustled budding leaves. He exhaled, the tension he didn't realize he'd been holding draining from his shoulders. Home.

George wasted no time in unloading. First came the groceries—he carried them into the cabin, careful not to track too much mud across the wooden floor. He placed the butter and milk in his small cooler box inside, a makeshift fridge that stayed chilly thanks to the still-cold nights. The coffee beans he set on the counter, planning to savor a fresh brew the next morning. He left the library books on his small reading table, eager to peruse them later.

Back outside, he fetched the spool of fishing line and bearings from the hardware store, storing them on his workbench. He also set aside the can of reel oil. Maybe he'd fix up his spinning reel after dinner. The rest of the items—some tinned goods, honey, and the jar of preserves—he put away systematically in his pantry corner. His cabin, though small, had everything arranged just so. A misplaced item could become a nuisance in a place where storage was at a premium.

With errands complete and supplies replenished, George felt a renewed sense of security. He made a simple pot of tea, sweetened with a dab of honey from the new jar, and carried a steaming cup to the front porch. The late-afternoon sun bathed the clearing in a warm glow. The forest seemed more vibrant than ever—a testament to spring's steady progress. He sipped slowly, reflecting on the day.

As he rested on the porch, the animals of the woods continued their routines. A single Chipmunk hopped across the clearing, pausing to sniff at a small tuft of grass. Overhead, a Red-tailed Hawk circled lazily, scanning for prey. George felt an inward relaxation that only came after returning to his solitary domain—this was his place of quiet reflection, the environment that anchored him. Though he'd enjoyed seeing Linda, Marlene, and Tim, he also appreciated the calm hush of the pines, the gentle lap of the lake's water just beyond the trees.

He was about to stand and retrieve his new bird guide when he heard a rustling near the edge of the clearing. Setting his teacup aside, he leaned forward. A young Deer—likely last year's fawn, now nearly grown—stepped cautiously into view. Its coat was a patchy mix of winter dullness and fresh spring color. Sensing no immediate threat, the Deer began foraging on emerging shoots near a patch of ferns. George watched, enthralled by the animal's poise. He wondered if it was one of the same fawns he'd glimpsed the previous autumn, grown bold enough now to venture closer to human structures.

He let out a slow breath, careful not to startle it. This, he thought, was the perfect testament to why he lived here—a quiet coexistence with the forest's denizens. The Deer's ears twitched at some distant sound, and after a minute of nibbling, it bounded away, white tail flashing. George remained still, a soft smile on his lips. In its own way, that fleeting visit felt like a welcome home.

As dusk crept in, he tidied the cabin, lit a small fire in the stove to ward off the chill, and prepared a light supper with some of the fresh groceries. He opted for a simple omelet, cracking two eggs from the newly purchased carton and adding a sprinkling of dried herbs. The sizzle in the pan mingled with the crackle of the fire. The meal tasted all the better knowing he had a pantry stocked with new basics—no more rationing coffee or scraping the last bits of flour.

After eating, he washed his dishes in a metal basin by the sink and dried them meticulously. Then he retrieved the library books from his reading table. First, he flipped through the new bird guide, marveling at the full-color photographs. A section on waterfowl caught his eye, so he studied the pages to see if there was any mention of unusual migratory patterns. He read about species that sometimes passed through northern lakes, imagining the chance to spot them as the season progressed.

Then, curiosity piqued, he cracked open the paperback novel by a local author. The opening lines described a fictional logging camp set in a forest much like the one surrounding his cabin, though from an earlier time. The style was simple but evocative, painting images of men felling great pines, guiding logs down rushing rivers. George found himself drawn in, comparing those fictional details to the real, subtle changes he'd seen in local waterways over the years.

Outside, the night deepened, the last traces of sunset fading into purple silhouettes beyond the treeline. Frogs began their chorus from the wetlands, joined by the occasional hoot of an owl. A gentle breeze rustled the eaves. George's eyelids grew heavy, lulled by the day's exertions and the comforting warmth of the cabin. He placed the novel aside, setting a bookmark in place.

Rising, he banked the stove's fire for the night, ensuring that if the temperature dropped, he wouldn't wake in a chill. Then he gathered his new spool of fishing line, deciding to do a bit of reel repair before turning in. But halfway through unscrewing the old bearings, he found himself yawning. The day's excitement—driving to town, socializing, loading groceries—had taken more out of him than he realized. He set the reel project aside, deciding to finish it in the morning when he was more alert.

He washed up, changed into soft flannel pajama pants, and climbed into his bunk, drawing the wool blanket over his legs. The glow from the stove bathed the cabin walls in shifting orange light.

He thought of Linda's café, Tim's hardware store, Mrs. Klinskey's library, and Marlene's warm smile at the general store. Despite his preference for solitude, these were people he cared about in his own quiet way—friendly faces who anchored the outskirts of his world. He felt a touch of gratitude for the small connections that brought meaning to life.

Lying there, listening to the frogs beyond the window, George reflected on how each trip to town reaffirmed both his ties to the community and his love for the forest. He never stayed away from the cabin for long, yet each visit to Kincaid Falls reminded him that he was part of a broader tapestry. It was an unspoken agreement: the townspeople respected his solitude, and in turn, he brought them stories of wildlife sightings and the taste of wilderness. He drifted off with that comforting thought, lulled by the steady hush of spring's night.

Tomorrow would bring fresh tasks: finishing the reel repair, maybe taking the canoe onto the lake for a test paddle. He'd also reorganize his pantry, ensuring the new supplies were properly stored. But for now, he let his mind settle into the present. The day's errands had been fruitful, the homecoming peaceful. In the gentle glow of dying embers, George closed his eyes and embraced the quiet contentment that came from knowing he had exactly what he needed: a stocked cabin, a welcoming town nearby, and the endless beauty of the north woods to keep him company.

7

PLEIN AIR PAINTING

Morning light filtered in through the cabin's windows, gentle and golden, as George awoke to the hush of an early summer day. Spring's frenetic energy was settling into the steadier rhythms of warmer weather—days of bright sunshine, occasional thunderstorms, and an explosion of green growth in every direction. When he stepped outside in the crisp, cool dawn, he could almost feel the forest breathing, alive with birdsong and new life. The earliest rays of sun fanned out across the lake, gilding its surface in shimmering gold.

For weeks, George had been gathering moments in his journal: the sight of trilliums carpeting the forest floor, the stirring of a black bear near his woodpile, the calls of coyotes skittering across the dusk. He had also tidied his small vegetable garden behind the cabin, planting onions, beans, and the last of his carrot seeds. Each day, the seedlings pushed higher, responding to the changing light and rising temperatures. A sense of soft contentment permeated everything he did.

Yet as much as George enjoyed the practical chores of cabin life, he felt a growing pull to return to one of his favorite pursuits—**plein air painting**. With the world in vibrant bloom, there was no better time to set up his easel along the lake's edge or in a forest clearing. All around him were landscapes bursting with color: the luminous greens of new leaves, the silver sheen of birch bark, the delicate pink or white blossoms that dotted certain shrubs. It was as though the entire north woods had decided to put on its finest attire after winter's starkness.

After breakfast—fried eggs and toast, with a small mug of black coffee—George set about collecting the items he'd need for a day of painting. His easel, a simple folding structure of worn wood and brass hinges, waited in a corner. He carefully inspected the legs, testing each joint to ensure it was still sturdy. Satisfied, he tucked it under his arm. Next came his canvas boards, some small, others medium-sized, all gesso-primed and ready to capture the colors of the north woods. He also gathered a small paint box containing tubes of oil paints, brushes of various shapes and sizes, and a jar of linseed oil. Finally, he slipped an old rag and a few cloths into the box for wiping brushes and cleaning up spills.

He dressed lightly in sturdy work pants and a faded flannel shirt with sleeves he could roll up if the midday sun proved too warm. A wide-brimmed hat hung on a peg by the door—he grabbed it on his way out, knowing the bright sun off the lake could be fierce. Slinging the paint box's strap across his shoulder, he lifted the easel in one hand and carried a small folding stool in the other. With a last glance around the cabin, he headed for the lake, boots scuffing lightly over the path.

Though the forest offered countless potential scenes—clusters of pines, mossy boulders, the interplay of light and shadow beneath tall maples—George found himself drawn to the lakeshore. He liked the interplay of water and sky, the reflection of clouds in the shifting surface, and the way the changing light danced across the shallows. Also, a mild breeze would keep some of the early summer insects at bay. Mosquitoes could be merciless this time of year, especially in still, shaded areas.

Stepping onto the small pebble beach, he surveyed the water. A loon called in the distance, its haunting cry echoing across the lake. A pair of ducks bobbed near an old beaver lodge, and the reeds along the shoreline swayed gently. The world felt wide and welcoming. Farther out, the morning sun backlit the rising mist, creating shifting veils of white that drifted across the surface like ghosts. George exhaled in appreciation. **This** was the moment he wanted to capture—this luminous hush between dawn and midmorning, when the sun still hung low enough to gild everything in gentle light.

He found a firm spot where the ground was mostly dry. Propping the easel legs in the sandy gravel, he adjusted them until the stand felt stable. Nearby, a young birch extended just enough shade to shield him if the day's heat grew strong. He set down his stool, balancing it on the uneven terrain. Then, from his paint box, he withdrew a small canvas board—maybe 9 by 12 inches—intending to work in a manageable size for his first plein air session of the season.

George's paint palette was a simple wooden rectangle with a thumb hole. He squeezed out small dabs of paint: titanium white, ultramarine blue, cerulean blue, cadmium yellow, yellow ochre, burnt umber, alizarin crimson, and a bit of sap green. These basic hues would allow him to mix any number of colors he needed. He used a small palette knife to blend them, preparing a few tints of blue and green for the water and trees. Next, he fashioned some gentle earth tones for the sandy shore and the distant tree line. He let himself linger over this preliminary step. There was something meditative about mixing paint in the open air, birds singing overhead, water lapping at the shore.

With a cloth rag in hand, he wiped a brush across a dollop of white paint, blending it with just enough cerulean and ochre to create a pale sky color. He liked to begin by sketching the major shapes in broad strokes—a horizon line, a suggestion of the forest background, and the gently sloping shore in the foreground. Every so often, he paused, scanning the scene before him. Clouds drifted across the sun, shifting the color of the water from bright blue to a softer gray-green. Plein air painting, he knew, demanded a certain dance with nature's changes. One could never expect the light to remain the same for long. The secret was to capture an impression, a feeling of the moment.

As George blocked in the composition, the painting took shape slowly. The top third of the canvas suggested a pale sky with hints of morning haze. Below that, he painted the lake in sweeping horizontal strokes—careful not to make the water too uniform. Nature thrived on subtle variations: a swirl of color where a small wave rippled, or a patch of deeper blue where the lake bed dropped off. He used a different brush for the shore, dabbing tans and browns for the rocky sand, adding flecks of green to suggest emerging weeds along the waterline.

Off to the left, the forest crowned the horizon—mostly pines with a scattering of hardwoods, all tinted in a tapestry of greens. He switched brushes, mixing sap green with a touch of yellow and white to replicate the vibrant new growth on some of the pines. For older, darker needles, he darkened his mixture with ultramarine and a bit of burnt umber. The interplay of warm and cool greens was mesmerizing. He felt the same delight that had struck him many times before: no matter how often he tried to paint the woods, they always offered fresh surprises, new color relationships, and endless variation.

He lost track of time in the best possible way. The sun inched higher, gilding the trees and sparking white highlights on the water. A gentle wind rustled the leaves, bringing the scent of pine resin and moist earth. A passing fish—or perhaps a muskrat—broke the surface of the lake, sending concentric ripples outward. George paused to observe, brush stilled midair. The ephemeral shapes on the water made him consider whether to add them into the scene, but he ultimately decided to keep the composition simpler. Plein air was about editing as much as capturing. One couldn't chase every fleeting detail.

Just as George refined the reflection of distant treetops in the water, he heard a faint rustle behind him. He turned to see a Fox stepping gingerly onto the shoreline a short distance away. It was a beautiful animal, its red coat sleek in the sunshine, bushy tail carried low. The Fox hesitated, noticing George, but it didn't flee. Instead, it stood still, dark eyes alert, ears twitching. For a long moment, the two regarded each other. George kept his movements slow, feeling a ripple of excitement at the proximity of wildlife. The Fox sniffed the air, then trotted closer to the water, lapping at the shallows.

George couldn't help but grin. He longed to reach for his camera, but it was tucked away inside the cabin, and any movement might send the Fox scurrying. So he simply watched, heart brimming with appreciation. After its drink, the Fox turned once more, gave him a quick glance, and then trotted off into the trees. The quiet hush it left behind seemed thicker than before. A parting gift, George thought, returning his attention to the canvas. He decided to place a faint suggestion of the Fox in the painting—a discreet shape along the shore, a mere brushstroke or two, as a personal nod to that fleeting encounter.

By late morning, the sun had crept high enough to warm the back of George's neck. Small beads of perspiration formed beneath his wide-brimmed hat. The bright light also made it trickier to accurately see the subtle colors on his palette. Deciding it was wise to rest, he set down his brush, stepped back from the easel, and scrutinized his progress. The painting captured the general mood of the lakeshore—the gentle slope of beach, the calm water reflecting a pale sky, and the distant green of the forest. But it still needed refining in certain areas, especially where the water met the shore. He jotted a mental note to fix the contrast once the paint settled a bit.

Reaching into his small rucksack, George retrieved a water bottle and a wrapped bundle of homemade bread and cheese. He settled on his folding stool, chewing slowly, eyes scanning the landscape. Clouds now drifted overhead, occasionally crossing the sun's path and casting the lake into a subdued hue. He considered how this shift might add depth to his work if he softened some of the highlights. The dynamic nature of plein air painting was both exhilarating and challenging—any moment's transformation of light could inspire a new brushstroke or a rethinking of color.

A brief breeze passed, bringing a swirl of warm air from across the lake. Dragonflies zipped over the water. In the reeds, a Bullfrog croaked, its deep resonant call undercutting the hum of insects. George found himself smiling at the layered tapestry of sounds. A day like this, open to possibility, reminded him why he'd chosen to live here. The forest, the lake, the wildlife—they gave him a sense of home that no city's bustle could replicate.

Once he finished lunch, George returned to his painting with renewed focus. The sun had drifted further west, lengthening the shadows. He decided to darken the tree line slightly to reflect the mid-afternoon light. Moving quickly, he mixed deeper greens and dabbed them into the background. Then he turned his attention to the water's surface, adding smaller, elongated reflections that would communicate the wind's subtle texture on the lake.

His brush danced across the canvas, layering translucent strokes of thinned paint over the earlier foundation. Thin glazes of ultramarine or phthalo green lent depth to sections of the water, while pale streaks of white brightened the sunlight's touch. He also refined the shore—a few staccato dots of sienna to suggest scattered pebbles, and a soft transitional zone where the shallow water revealed the sandy bottom.

On the lower left edge of the painting, he placed a small shape of russet and gray, barely more than a few dabs with a fine brush. This hint of the Fox's presence felt whimsical, a personal memory embedded in the scene. He doubted anyone else would notice it at first glance, but that was the nature of his art—layered with personal significance, as well as natural beauty.

From time to time, he stood up to stretch, stepping back several paces. Gauging the painting from a distance helped him see issues of proportion or color balance that were invisible up close. He sipped water, wiped his brow, then dug back in, adjusting and refining. The afternoon passed in a calm, focused rhythm. A pair of squirrels raced along the branches behind him. Somewhere upstream, a Beaver slapped its tail on the water, but George didn't see it. He was deeply immersed in the interplay of shape and color.

In late afternoon, the sky began to shift again. Distant clouds gathered on the western horizon, tinged with faint grays and the potential for an early summer storm. A mild drop in temperature made the hairs on George's arms stand up. He paused his painting to scan the skies. It wasn't unusual this time of year for a pop-up thunderstorm to form, delivering a sudden downpour and then passing on. He debated whether to keep painting or to pack up before the weather turned.

Deciding to press on a bit longer, he added more dynamic shading to the clouds in his sky portion, capturing something of the day's evolution. The gently swirling shapes shifted from the initial morning brightness to a layered, slightly more ominous tone. He was mindful, though, that oil paint could only absorb so much continuous layering in a single session. If the sky turned truly dark, he might have to let the painting dry and resume it another day.

Sure enough, within half an hour, a soft rumble of thunder carried over the lake. George felt a subtle electric charge in the air. Over the forest canopy to the west, the sky glowed a pale greenish-gray, a sure sign of impending rain. He took stock of his progress. The painting had reached a point of near-completion—at least for a first plein air session. Another hour or two of detail work might be ideal in perfect conditions, but nature had its own schedule.

He packed away his brushes and paints methodically, wiping each brush clean with a rag and swirling it in a small jar of mineral spirits. Then he carefully stowed his palette, making sure not to smear his fresh mixes all over the inside of the paint box. Gently, he lifted the canvas board off the easel. The oil paint was still wet, so he slipped it into a small carrying frame he'd built to protect drying canvases. A gust of wind flapped the edges of his shirt, carrying the scent of rain and ozone. With the painting secure, he folded up his easel and stool.

No sooner had George turned toward the cabin than the first drops fell, large and heavy. They splatted on the sandy shore, sending tiny bursts of dust and forming dark spots that spread quickly. He tucked the painting protectively under one arm, pulling his hat low over his brow. In minutes, the sprinkle escalated to a downpour, and the sky unleashed its pent-up energy. Sheets of rain splashed across the lake, flattening the surface into a gray churn. Thunder boomed more insistently.

George broke into a brisk walk—almost a jog—hustling back through the path. The towering pines overhead offered partial cover, but the storm was too strong to keep him dry. By the time he spotted the cabin's familiar outline, he was soaked from the waist down. He laughed at the spectacle, though—this sudden shift from serene painting session to a sprint in a drenching storm felt quintessentially northern. Nature never shied from reminding him who was in charge.

He made it to the porch, heart pumping. The wooden steps were slick under the onslaught of rainwater. He placed the easel and stool inside first, then gingerly maneuvered the canvas box and the wet painting into the dry interior. Once everything was safe, he shut the door and peeled off his wet shirt, flinging droplets onto the floor. He toweled himself off quickly, then changed into a fresh flannel and set his soggy garments near the stove to dry.

The storm raged outside, drumming on the cabin's roof with impressive force. Flashes of lightning lit up the windows, followed by resonant booms of thunder rolling across the lake. Despite the storm's intensity, the cabin felt cozy and secure. George had built it with sturdy logs years ago, ensuring it could withstand harsh northern winters and violent summer tempests alike. He stoked the fire in the woodstove, not for warmth—since the air was still mild—but to chase away the dampness. A soft glow bathed the cabin, merging with the flickers of lightning outside.

He placed the wet canvas board on a small drying shelf near a window where it could receive some indirect light. Then he took a moment to admire his work. Though the paint was still wet, he could see the interplay of colors he'd created—the subtle gradient of the sky, the shining water, the forested shore. Perhaps in a day or two, once it set enough, he'd revisit the painting for final touches in the cabin or carry it outside again. He felt a surge of contentment; capturing that lakeshore scene had fulfilled a creative longing deep within him.

Next, George prepared a quick meal to ward off the hunger that had crept in during his afternoon of painting. He chopped some root vegetables— carrots, onions, and a few potatoes—tossed them into a cast-iron pot with broth, and set it on the stove to simmer. While the soup cooked, he settled in his rocking chair, listening to the rain lash the windows. The onslaught ebbed and surged in waves. Thunder rumbled continuously, a rolling bass note that resonated in his chest. He felt a primal thrill at the storm's energy, grateful he could watch it unfold from a place of safety.

As the minutes wore on, the thunder's intervals grew longer, the rain softened, and the roar on the roof quieted to a patter. Steam rose from the pot of soup, carrying a savory aroma through the cabin. George ladled a portion into a bowl, sprinkled a pinch of salt, and sat at his small wooden table. Each spoonful tasted of warmth and nourishment.

Between bites, he glanced over at the painting, thinking of the Fox that had briefly graced his morning. He wondered where the creature might be sheltering now—perhaps under a thick canopy of fir trees or an overhang of rock.

By the time he finished his meal and washed the dishes, the storm had mostly passed. Curious, George opened the front door to step onto his porch. The air felt cooler, cleansed by the torrent of rain, and the sky had begun to clear. Rays of late-day sunlight broke through tattered clouds, painting the forest in a brilliant post-storm glow. A rainbow arced faintly over the eastern horizon, spanning the lake in a gentle curve of color.

Enchanted by the sight, George couldn't resist stepping barefoot into the damp grass. The ground squelched under his toes, reminding him how quickly the weather had changed. The lake, now calm again, mirrored the pinks and purples of the twilight sky. Droplets clung to the leaves of every plant, catching the waning sun's glow like tiny jewels. He breathed in deeply, the scent of wet pine needles and fresh earth filling his senses. Moments like this, he thought, deserved quiet gratitude.

A humming calm settled over the woods. Tree frogs began their evening chorus, layered with the occasional drip of leftover rainwater falling from branches. George ambled around the clearing, letting the last warmth of the day soak into his skin. He discovered small pools where rain had collected in footprints, reflecting miniature skies. In the fading light, he spotted a few deer tracks along the path near the water's edge, a sign they had ventured close during or just after the storm.

When twilight gave way to dusk, George returned inside, lit a lantern, and sat at his writing desk. He opened his journal to a fresh page, the paper tinted golden under the lantern's glow. Outside, the nighttime forest grew more vocal by the minute—frogs, crickets, the soft rustle of leaves. He put pen to paper, capturing the day's experiences:

June 2nd: Began plein air painting near the lakeshore—first time this year. Morning light was perfect. Captured the reflection of pines on the water. A Fox appeared, drinking at the shore. Painted a small shape of it into the scene, a reminder of the visit. Afternoon storm arrived quickly. Rushed home soaked, but painting stayed safe. Thunder was magnificent—cabin remained warm and dry. After the storm, the rainbow over the lake was a blessing. The forest glowed, reborn in fresh color.

He paused, tapping the pen thoughtfully. The day had felt almost magical in its harmony of creative effort and natural beauty, culminating in that dramatic storm. He added a final reflection:

Painting the lake in real time is always a dance with the shifting light. No two hours look the same. I aim not for perfection but for a truthful impression—how the morning felt in that singular moment, the hush of dawn and the hush in my heart.

With that, he closed the journal, letting the ink dry. The storm had cooled the air enough that he considered lighting a small, low fire again, but the cabin remained comfortable. Instead, he extinguished the lantern, letting the moonlight outside create soft patterns on the floor. He stood by the window, hands folded, gazing at the silvered lake. The moon shone through thinning clouds, and stars began to poke through overhead. It was a night for quiet wonder.

The hour grew late, and George climbed into his bunk, pulling a light blanket across his legs. The cabin settled into its nocturnal symphony—the gentle cracking of wood as it cooled, the faint drip of water rolling off the eaves, and the persistent hum of frogs calling through the open window. His mind drifted over the day's images: the half-finished painting, the rustle of the Fox, the sudden curtain of rain. Each memory glowed with a vitality that only came from full immersion in nature's cadence.

Before sleep claimed him, he thought of the next day's plans. Perhaps he'd spend the morning touching up the new painting indoors, where the light through the window would remain steady. Or maybe he'd venture to a different part of the lakeshore to capture a fresh angle. Summertime always brought him endless subject matter—wildflowers in bloom, the shifting tapestry of clouds, the interplay of shade beneath towering pines. The act of painting outdoors—en plein air—was not just a hobby for George; it was a way to slow down and truly see the land he cherished.

As he drifted off, the memory of brush against canvas and the hush of water lapping at his feet danced in his thoughts. He held a quiet conviction that tomorrow, or the day after, or the day after that, he'd return to the lakeshore with his easel. He'd keep wrestling with the ever-changing light, trying to capture the smallest fraction of the forest's immensity, one brushstroke at a time. In this gentle pursuit, he found endless satisfaction, each painting a testament to the subtle wonders of life in the woods.

Outside, moonlight silvered the lake and the pines stood like silent guardians. Inside, the cabin glowed with the embers of day's contentment. Soon, his slow, steady breathing merged with the forest's nighttime lullaby. Another chapter of early summer passed into memory, and George, painter and keeper of solitude, slept peacefully, ready to greet the dawn and the blank canvas of a new day.

8

SUMMER FLY FISHING

Summer announced its arrival in the north woods with a gentle nudge rather than a dramatic flourish. One morning, George simply realized the cool edge of spring had vanished from the air. Days were long, the sun rising early and lingering past dinner, drenching the forest in light that seemed to last forever. The nights grew balmy and hummed with life. Frogs trilled in the wetlands near the cabin, while a thousand insects joined in a high-pitched chorus that lulled George to sleep. The lake, once thick with ice and then softly thawed in spring, now gleamed under the summer sky, inviting him to paddle and fish whenever the mood struck. His little vegetable garden behind the cabin overflowed with leafy greens, onions, and bright flowers that promised a bounty of produce in the coming weeks. Everywhere he looked, growth and vitality reigned.

Most mornings, George woke at dawn, drew a cup of coffee, and stood on his porch to watch the sun break over the treetops. The forest shimmered in a haze of gold, dew clinging to ferns and undergrowth. He was always struck by how silent the world felt at that early hour, even though he knew the hush was an illusion—countless living creatures were already stirring, readying themselves for the day's hunt or forage. By the time he finished his coffee, the veil lifted. Birdsong arose in earnest, joined by the gentle breeze rattling leaves and the far-off splash of a Beaver tail slapping the water's surface. It was in these moments, breathing in the fresh green scent of summer, that George felt most deeply content. Life in the woods moved at a pace he could understand, measured by shifting light, the tilt of the sun, and the rustle of wildlife along the edges of the clearing.

Fly fishing beckoned to him especially now. Though he'd tried his hand at everything from ice fishing to simple bobber rigs, it was the artful flick of a fly rod that truly captured his imagination, especially in the heat of summer. Fly fishing demanded a slow, deliberate approach—reading the water, matching the hatch, tying the right pattern to mimic whichever insects hovered near the lake's surface. In winter, he'd spent hours tying flies by his fireplace, carefully attaching bits of feather and fur to hooks, imagining how trout or bass might respond. Now was the season to test those creations. The lake's shallows teemed with Largemouth and Smallmouth Bass in pursuit of dragonflies, damselflies, and all manner of aquatic larvae. Even Walleye and the occasional Musky might show interest in a well-presented fly.

On a bright, calm morning in mid-June, George loaded his canoe with the essentials: a light fly rod, a small tackle box stuffed with hand-tied flies, a landing net, and a thermos of cold water. He also brought along his camera and an old straw hat to shield him from the sun's glare. Pushing off from the stony shoreline felt like stepping into another realm. The lake was glass-still, reflecting the sky so perfectly that paddling across its surface seemed like rowing through a dream. Only the ripples from his canoe disturbed that mirror. A loon called in the distance, and George paused to watch it dive, leaving an expanding ring of water behind. When it vanished, the surface grew tranquil once again. He dipped his paddle slowly, heading for a secluded bay he knew well—a place where lily pads thrived and bass often lurked beneath the green canopy of floating leaves.

He set down the paddle and let the canoe drift. An early sun illuminated the bay's edges, revealing underwater logs and weed beds where fish might hide. The water was surprisingly clear for midsummer; he could see small Bluegills darting around, scouting for morsels. Taking his rod, George stood carefully. He stripped a few feet of line from the reel, then flicked the rod tip to send the line forward in smooth arcs. Each false cast shimmered in the golden light. With a final push, he laid the fly—a fuzzy popper patterned to look like a distressed dragonfly—onto the water's surface. It landed with a delicate *plop*, floating amid the lily pads. For a moment, nothing happened. Then, a swirl disturbed the stillness. A shape moved below. The popper twitched. Adrenaline coursed through George. He gave the line a gentle tug, making the fly dance.

Suddenly, a bass struck, sending a splash of water into the warm morning air. George reacted by lifting the rod, feeling the line go taut and the rod bend. The fish peeled away under the lily pads, and George let the line slip through his fingers to avoid breaking it. He could see the swirl of green and silver under the surface—definitely a Largemouth by its markings. Carefully, he applied pressure, coaxing it away from the snags. The bass jumped once, glistening in the sunlight, then dove again. George grinned, heart pounding. It wasn't the largest fish he'd ever caught, but the excitement of a topwater strike never grew old. Within minutes, he guided it to the canoe and used his net to scoop it up. The fish's sides heaved, water dripping from vibrant scales. With quiet appreciation, he removed the barbless hook, admiring the healthy creature. He took a moment to tip his hat in salute before releasing it back into the water.

That release was always a highlight for George—watching the fish vanish into the aquatic realm from which it came. He saw it as a small exchange, a momentary intrusion into the fish's world, balanced by letting the creature go free. With the day still young, he continued exploring the bay, casting beneath overhanging branches, near sunken logs, and into pockets of lily pads. He picked up another bass or two, along with a feisty Bluegill that hit his popper with the ferocity of a creature twice its size. More than once, he found himself laughing aloud at the tiny fish's boldness. When the sun rose overhead, turning the gentle breeze into a thicker, lazier warmth, he paddled back to the shore, satisfied with his morning's efforts.

Returning to the cabin, George set his fishing gear to dry, the canoe resting upside-down to drain any water that had splashed inside. Summer's midday heat now wrapped around everything, and he decided to pour a glass of iced tea made from wild mint and a bit of honey. He sat on his porch, letting the hush of afternoon lull him. This was a time he often used for reflection or simpler chores, leaving the more strenuous tasks for morning or evening when temperatures were cooler. He thought back to the earlier part of the year—how the forest had been locked in ice, the crisp hush of winter dominating every corner of his life. Now, that memory felt like another world. The sun had banished all traces of cold, and the forest teemed with insects, birds, chipmunks, even snakes occasionally slithering through the undergrowth.

Later that afternoon, he found himself at his fly-tying table once again. Even though he had enough flies for the season, he enjoyed experimenting with new patterns. He pinned a small hook into his vise, selecting bright yellow deer hair, a bit of red chenille, and some flashy tinsel. Something about the combination struck him as ideal for a late-summer lure—maybe for catching the bigger Smallmouth that roamed the rocky points. He worked methodically: first winding the thread, then tying in each material, building a shape that mimicked a popper or a terrestrial insect. As he tied, he could hear the buzz of wasps outside and the occasional slap of a Beaver tail echoing from the lake. The cabin's windows were wide open, letting in a gentle cross-breeze. The temperature was hot enough that he wore only a light short-sleeved shirt, but within the shaded log walls, it felt comfortably cool.

Evening brought a cooler gust across the water, stirring the tall pines. George decided to fish once more, this time for the dusk bite that sometimes lured bigger bass toward the shallows. He readied the same canoe, though now the sky glowed with tints of pink and orange as the sun dipped low. The day's heat relented, replaced by the hush of twilight. Drifting out into the lake, he noticed the water's surface reflecting the sky so vividly that it felt like paddling through a painting. Skeins of insects hovered near the reeds, turning the air above them into a shimmering mass. A Kingfisher swooped overhead, rattling a sharp cry before perching on a dead limb to watch for small fish.

He aimed for a rocky point he'd visited many times in autumn. Summer changed the vegetation, and the submerged rocks often hosted crayfish—a favorite meal for Smallmouth Bass. He swapped his topwater popper for a handmade crayfish pattern, sinking it near the bottom with a slow retrieve. The line went tight just as the last sunlight slipped behind the horizon. A strong fish surged, bending his rod. This time, the fight felt heavier, with the fish darting unpredictably in deeper water. George let out a laugh of surprise, bracing against the gunwale as the canoe swayed. He played the fish patiently, guiding it away from submerged snags. With a final surface swirl, a plump Smallmouth emerged, broad and bronze, shimmering with red eyes. Using both hands, he brought it alongside, slipping the landing net beneath. The fish, maybe two pounds, exuded raw strength. George removed the hook gently, took a brief second to appreciate its bold coloring, and set it free. Its tail flicked water in a farewell splash.

Satisfied, he paddled home in the deepening dusk. Fireflies danced near the shoreline, flickering points of light that turned the forest edge into a nightly festival. Overhead, the first stars appeared. He navigated by memory, the lake so calm it felt like glass. The moon, still low, cast a faint glow across the water. By the time he reached his cabin, the world was a tapestry of nocturnal sounds. Crickets and frogs led the symphony, joined by the distant hoot of an owl. After securing his canoe, he climbed onto his porch and gazed up at the stars that glinted between tall treetops. A mild breeze whispered past, cooling the sweat on his brow. Days like these—beginning with dawn's golden hush and ending in star-spangled calm—reminded him why he had chosen a life of simplicity and closeness to nature.

Inside, he lit his lantern. The cabin glowed with soft light, casting dancing shadows across the log walls. He prepared a small supper of fresh greens and a modest portion of bread, finishing it off with a cup of tea. While he ate, he recounted the day's events in his journal: the swirling fish in the lily pads, the Kingfisher's rattling cry, the moment the Smallmouth hammered his crayfish pattern. He sketched a quick outline of the fish in the margin, capturing the proud tilt of its dorsal fin. Then he wrote a few lines about the water's temperature, the wind direction, and the subtle changes in insect hatches he'd noticed—small details that might prove valuable on a future trip, or that might simply enrich his memories years from now.

As summer deepened, George varied his fishing spots and techniques. Some mornings, he tramped through the woods to a smaller, hidden lake where Brook Trout lurked in cooler waters. Other days, he portaged his canoe to a chain of interconnected lakes that led deep into the wilderness, searching for Lake Trout that might still linger in the depths. Occasionally, he targeted Walleye around twilight, using a sinking line and a minnow-imitating fly near weed beds. The fish became more active after sundown, and sometimes, hooking into a Walleye by fly rod in near darkness felt like conjuring a small miracle. The nights dripped with moonlight, and the forest around him thrummed with quiet energy.

Not all outings were successful. At times, the fish refused to bite, or a sudden weather shift shut down their feeding. George accepted these moments calmly. After all, fishing was only partly about the catch. It was also about the hush of the lake at dawn, the swirl of a breeze through pines, the sudden quiet that fell when a predator—like a Bald Eagle—soared overhead. There were times he spent hours casting without so much as a nibble, yet he returned to the cabin with a sense of peace, having lost himself in the rhythmic flick of the fly line and the shimmering reflections of the forest.

On sultry afternoons when the sun blazed high, he sometimes took a break from fishing to swim in the lake's deeper sections. Paddling the canoe to a small rocky outcrop, he'd strip to his shorts and ease into the water, relishing the cool embrace that banished the heat. He'd float on his back, letting the sunshine spangle his face, listening to his own breath mingling with the whisper of water against stone. Afterwards, he'd stretch out on the rocks like a contented turtle, drying off in the warm breeze. The air smelled of sunbaked pine needles and sweet grass, the lake lapping at the shore below.

In the cabin during the evenings, after enjoying a simple meal—perhaps pan-fried fish if he'd chosen to keep one for dinner—he settled by the open window with a book or his journal. The last light of day painted the inside of the cabin in soft amber. Once that glow faded, the lantern or a single candle provided just enough illumination to read by. Moths fluttered outside the window screen, drawn by the faint glimmer within. George sometimes paused his reading to glance up and see their pale wings tapping at the screen, attracted to the flame. The gentle hush enveloped him—no television, no hum of electricity, only the crackle of the fire in his stove and the night chorus beyond.

On one particularly bright morning, George decided to bring his camera along for a day's fishing. It was a modest camera, older but reliable, capable of capturing the essence of the woods in all their summertime glory. He tucked it into a waterproof bag in the canoe. After a successful run of hooking Smallmouth Bass on the lake's rocky drop-offs, he paddled toward a secluded cove filled with drifting lilies. The water was shallow and looked almost untouched. On a whim, he cast his line along the lily edge, hoping a sunning Largemouth might strike. Instead, what emerged was not a fish but a small family of beavers. They paddled leisurely across the cove, their flat tails slicing through the water in quiet unison.

Moving slowly, George set his rod aside and reached for the camera. He snapped several frames as the beavers swam. One adult carried a leafy branch in its mouth, presumably for a lodge repair or a meal. The younger beavers swam close, occasionally bumping into each other in what looked like playful curiosity. George felt a smile tug at his beard. He'd encountered beavers many times, but each sighting charmed him anew, offering a glimpse into their steady, industrious world. When they finally submerged, leaving only ripples behind, he pocketed the camera and resumed fishing, heart warmed by the gentle spectacle.

Summer also brought a sprinkling of thunderstorms, often rolling in with little warning. On a few occasions, the afternoon sky darkened dramatically while George was out on the lake, forcing him to paddle home quickly as lightning forked in the distance. He'd tie up the canoe, retreat indoors, and wait out the storm by the fireplace, the cabin walls echoing with thunder's rumble. Rain hammered the roof, turning the clearing into a sparkling, dripping world once the storm passed. Inevitably, the air felt cleaner afterwards, the leaves glistening, the mosquitoes out in force. Fishing right after a storm could be sublime if the water didn't muddy, as certain fish became more active in the cooler, oxygen-rich conditions.

Whenever he kept a fish for a meal, he treated it with respect, cleaning it carefully on his porch and disposing of scraps far from the cabin to avoid attracting unwelcome wildlife. He found that fresh-caught bass or walleye, cooked in a little butter with herbs from his garden, offered some of the finest eating imaginable. A simple side of roasted potatoes or a salad of leafy greens completed the feast. At times, he'd reflect on the old adage that "food tastes best when you've worked for it," and he'd grin, thinking of the hours spent perfecting cast after cast, or trekking across portages to remote lakes. Everything about such a meal reminded him of his place in the natural cycle.

By mid-summer, the forest around him was lush to the point of extravagance. Grasses and wildflowers swayed in the meadows, while ferns grew waist-high in the shade. Deer visited the edges of his clearing, nibbling at tender shoots. Now and then, he glimpsed a black bear lumbering through the woods in search of berries. As long as he kept his food secured, the bear rarely lingered. In these months, the nights remained mild, and he often left his windows open to enjoy the nocturnal hum. Some nights, the call of Loons on the lake drifted directly into his dreams, lending them a haunting, comforting melody.

A certain equilibrium had taken hold, bridging man and wilderness. George saw how the fish fed on emerging insects, how the birds hunted those same insects, and how the entire forest thrived in a delicate chain of life. He was but one participant in that chain, reliant on the land for sustenance and meaning. The small rituals—tying a new fly, scanning the water for subtle signs of fish activity, listening for the wind's direction—grounded him more deeply with each passing day. Whenever he tried to articulate that connection in his journal, words felt too shallow. It was better expressed in the swirl of water around a lure, or the hush that fell when a heron took flight across the marsh.

As July inched toward August, the sun lingered in the sky, and evenings glowed with a slower, honeyed light. On one golden evening, George found himself sitting by the lake after a short fishing session. He'd caught and released a half-dozen spirited bass, feeling no need to keep any. With his rod propped nearby, he simply gazed across the water. A gentle breeze brushed his hair, carrying the scent of warm pine needles. The forest's reflection lay on the lake's surface in liquid clarity. Dragonflies skimmed the surface, leaving tiny ripples.

He thought of the seasons he'd witnessed in this very spot—snow banks towering in winter, the crackle of ice shifting beneath his boots, the slow re-emergence of green each spring. Now, amid the peak of summer's fullness, it felt as though the land breathed with a calm, steady pulse. He took it all in: the mesmerizing hush, the last rays of sun catching dust motes in the air, the symphony of frogs and crickets ramping up for their nightly performance. Eventually, the sun dipped below the horizon, painting the sky in pastel pinks and purples. The water faded to a deeper blue, and the hush grew profound.

At last, George gathered his rod, slipped into his canoe, and paddled back toward his cabin. Fireflies winked among the pines, and the moon began its ascent, pale and shy in the early night. He felt no hurry. Summer's warm and languid days gifted him with the luxury of unhurried time. The swirl of the paddle in the lake, the drip of water off the blade, and the gentle rocking of the canoe formed an unspoken lullaby. On shore, he pulled the canoe up and walked to his porch, where the lantern's soft glow waited.

Inside, he lit a small fire in the stove for ambiance more than warmth. He changed into comfortable clothes and washed his hands in a basin, the water still faintly cool from the spring that fed his cabin. Then, by lamplight, he jotted down the day's notes in his journal—how the Bass had struck at dawn, how the clouds shifted midafternoon, how the insects danced at dusk. Each entry formed a mosaic of summer life in the woods, small puzzle pieces that captured the fleeting nature of each day. And in so doing, he knew he was preserving these experiences, not only for himself but perhaps for whoever might read his scribbled lines in the future.

The hour grew late. He stifled a yawn, closed his journal, and snuffed the lantern. The cabin dimmed to a gentle darkness lit only by moonbeams from the window. Outside, the forest pulsed with secret life: raccoons foraging, owls gliding silently in search of prey, deer tiptoeing through meadows drenched in moonlight. George climbed into his bunk, the sound of his heartbeat merging with the hush of the woods. Tomorrow might bring a new fishing venture or perhaps a day spent painting, or maybe just quiet reflection on the porch. But for now, warm summer air and the promise of restful sleep enveloped him. It was enough to be here, at peace with the land and water, cradled by the gentle embrace of a northern summer.

So ended another day in George's life by the lake—a day of sunlit waters and dancing dragonflies, of vibrant fish and quiet revelations, of the world in full summer bloom. In the silence of the cabin, with the forest's lullaby in his ears, he drifted into dreams, a gentle smile lingering beneath his thick gray beard. The north woods carried on, shimmering in starlight, content with the rhythm of a season that knew no hurry and offered, for those who chose to look, an endless invitation into nature's timeless dance.

9

HIKING AND CAMPING TRIPS

Morning in the north woods found George sitting at his small table, thoughtfully studying a forest map spread before him. Sunlight angled through the cabin's windows in bright golden beams, illuminating the creases on the map where it had been folded and refolded over the years. Every tear and coffee stain told a tale of trails wandered, summits climbed, and hidden lakes discovered. He sipped his usual black coffee, letting the steam curl around his thick gray beard. Summer had reached its glorious peak—long days of radiant sun, nights buzzing with insects, and the forest brimming with life. There was no better time, George decided, for a true backcountry camping trip.

He ran a finger along a faint line that snaked away from the eastern edge of the lake. The route meandered through dense stands of spruce, skirted rolling hills of birch and maples, and eventually wound into a tract of wilderness marked by higher elevations—rugged country rarely visited except by the most determined hikers. He'd been there years ago, back when his beard was still more salt-and-pepper than silver-gray. His memory of that trip glowed with images of clear streams, rocky ridges with sweeping views, and nights spent under a sky jeweled with stars. Now, he felt the pull again, as if the land itself were calling him to revisit those winding trails and secret groves.

Outside, the cabin yard buzzed with summer's activity. A hummingbird zipped past the porch, investigating the wildflowers that George had transplanted near the steps. He stood to gather his gear, methodically assembling items on the bunk: a sturdy pack, sleeping bag, compact tent, cooking pot, canteen, and enough dried foods to last several days. He planned to fish for extra protein—both to lighten his pack and to immerse himself more fully in the wilderness's gifts. Along with the essentials, he included a well-worn journal, a small watercolor kit, and his camera, determined to document the journey and capture any fleeting, wondrous moments.

When all was ready, George stepped onto the porch, inhaling the scents of pine resin and warm earth. He locked the cabin door, though in truth, few ventured this far into the woods. Then he adjusted the straps of his pack, grabbed his walking stick—carved from a sturdy branch of ash—and began his trek. Early sunlight dappled the trail, and a chorus of birdsong followed him into the forest's cool embrace.

Initially, the trail felt familiar. The pine-needle carpet muffled his footsteps, and bright shafts of morning light filtered between branches overhead. He walked steadily, letting his body settle into a rhythm. Summer flowers bloomed along the edges—pale blue harebells, yellow hawkweed, and the occasional stand of fireweed with its magenta blossoms. Where winter's silence had once dominated, the forest now rustled with life: squirrels chasing each other up trees, chipmunks darting across the path, bees droning amid wildflowers. The air, though still fresh, carried a hint of midday warmth to come.

After an hour or so, he paused to refill his canteen at a small stream. Clear water trickled over stones, shining in the sun. Kneeling on the bank, George cupped his hands, bringing the cool liquid to his lips. It tasted of pure snowmelt filtered through rich soil—an essence of the land. He splashed some on his face, relishing the bracing chill, then filled his canteen. A flash of movement caught his eye upstream: a trout flicked through the shallows, vanishing in a swirl. George smiled, making a mental note to cast a line there on his return. For now, the day's hike awaited.

Pressing on, he veered east where the path diverged, leaving behind the more frequented trails near the lake. The going became more rugged. Fallen trees lay across the track, forcing him to climb or detour. Branches snatched at his pack. Every so often, he paused to consult the map, verifying his course by the shapes of ridges and valleys. The forest thickened, and a hush seemed to deepen. He kept an eye out for wildlife—perhaps a Moose browsing near a bog, or a Black Bear lured by berries. He carried a small canister of bear spray, always mindful of surprising an animal at close range. Still, he found comfort in nature's unpredictability, trusting his instincts honed by years of living here.

By midday, the sun's heat intensified. Golden beams slanted through the canopy, warming the undergrowth until the forest exuded a heady, green scent. George felt perspiration trickle down his back, and his breath came more labored. At a small clearing, he stopped to rest. A fallen log provided a seat, half-covered in moss and bracket fungi. He shrugged off his pack, took a long pull of water, and unwrapped a pouch of dried venison and crackers.

While he ate, he watched a pair of butterflies dance in the filtered light, their wings a swirl of orange and black. The hush of midday hush enveloped him, broken only by an occasional birdcall.

A sense of peace settled over him—this was precisely why he had come. The rigors of hiking, the immersion in green shadows and gentle breezes, the flutter of life all around. The demands of daily chores back at the cabin fell away. He lingered a while, nibbling and refilling his lungs with fresh forest air, until the urge to move on tugged him again.

The topography changed as the trail climbed into higher ground. Granite outcroppings jutted from the forest floor, draped in lichen and softened by moss. Birch and maple gave way to stands of fir and spruce, their needles scenting the air with a crisp tang. The path narrowed, sometimes little more than a thread between boulders. But George welcomed the challenge. His legs, used to hours of fishing and canoe portaging, responded well. He pressed onward, though he took care to place each footfall securely on the uneven terrain.

During one steep ascent, he paused to catch his breath, heart thrumming from exertion. Turning, he glimpsed a partial view of the land below: an endless sea of treetops, the shimmering line of the lake glimpsed far in the distance. Clouds drifted overhead in slow white sails, and the sun burnished everything in bright midafternoon light. He wiped sweat from his brow, a grin forming beneath his beard. This place, remote and ancient, felt like a cathedral of pines and granite, a timeless realm where humans were guests at best.

He pushed on until he crested a small ridge that overlooked a hidden valley. The terrain dipped into a lush basin overshadowed by taller hills. A trickle of water carved through the center, forming a shallow pond. In winter, it would freeze solid, but now, in high summer, it glistened with life—cattails, lily pads, and the gentle hum of dragonflies. George recalled that a spur trail to the south could lead to an upland meadow, another scenic spot. But for tonight, the valley was enough. Already, he imagined a suitable campsite among the tall pines near the pond.

He descended carefully, picking his way down the slope. At the valley floor, he found a level patch of ground shielded by spruce. A flat rock jutted beside the pond, perfect for cooking or stargazing later. The area seemed well away from any major game trails—useful for avoiding unexpected nighttime visitors. A quick scan confirmed no obvious signs of recent bear or moose. Satisfied, he shrugged off his pack and began setting up camp.

In the hush of midafternoon, George pitched his compact tent. The process was routine, like greeting an old friend. He'd used this same durable shelter for countless excursions. Once the tent was staked, he spread his sleeping pad and bag inside, tucking them neatly away. Next, he cleared a small area for a fire ring, arranging a circle of stones. Although it was warm, a fire would provide light and help keep insects at bay. He gathered fallen branches for tinder—never cutting fresh wood, out of respect for the forest's living trees.

As he worked, a flicker of movement caught his eye across the pond. Carefully, he looked up to see a doe stepping from the shadows. Her ears flicked, scanning the area. She bent to sip from the water, lapping gently at the pond's edge. George froze, enthralled by the graceful lines of her body, the tension in each sinew. In that moment, the hush of the valley felt absolute. Even the birds seemed to hold their breath, as if acknowledging the deer's presence. Slowly, he reached for his camera but hesitated. Some encounters, he felt, were better left unrecorded by technology. Instead, he simply watched until the doe lifted her head, caught his scent on the breeze, and melted back into the trees with a single fluid motion.

George exhaled, marveling at how privileged he felt to witness such moments. These were the gifts of wilderness—moments of communion that reminded him of his place in the grand tapestry of life. He gathered the last of his firewood, set the pieces near the ring, and decided to explore the pond's edge a bit before twilight.

A gentle hush draped the valley as the sun dipped behind the ridges. Shadows stretched across the water, and a chorus of frogs began their nightly serenade, accompanied by the hum of mosquitoes. George rubbed a dab of insect repellent on his exposed arms, then took up his fly rod. The pond looked shallow enough that casting near the lilies might yield a feisty Brook Trout or even a bass. He tied on a small nymph pattern, one he'd created specifically for still waters. The vantage of the water's surface, nearly mirror-like in the fading light, filled him with anticipation.

He waded a few steps from the bank, boots sinking into soft muck. On his second cast, a gentle tug answered his offering. He lifted the rod, heart skipping. The line tightened, and a small trout broke the surface, dancing in the golden last rays of sun. The fish was no more than eight inches, but its colors glowed—a mosaic of red spots and pale halos on a tawny background. George reeled it in swiftly, cradling it in wet hands. The trout's gills flared in the cool air, eyes wide. This was dinner, if he chose. But with quick, careful movements, he slipped the barbless hook free and released the fish back into the pond. Tonight, he decided, a simple meal of dried provisions would suffice. A single fish might not fill him anyway, and he felt more gratitude in letting it swim another day.

He cast a few more times without luck, then retreated to shore as dusk gathered. Fireflies began their nightly dance, winking over the water's surface like floating sparks. George ignited a small fire in the ring of stones and placed a pot of water to boil. Once it bubbled, he mixed in dehydrated vegetables, rice, and a packet of seasoning. The aroma soon drifted around camp, and he realized how hungry he'd become after the day's hiking. He ate slowly, savoring each spoonful by firelight, occasionally pausing to listen for any rustling beyond the glow. At one point, the crack of a branch echoed through the valley, making him glance sharply into the darkness. Perhaps a raccoon or fox prowled near. He reminded himself to stash all food securely after the meal.

By the time he cleaned up, the stars shone in full glory overhead. Pale light from the waxing moon illuminated the tops of tall spruce. He poured himself a cup of tea, steeped from a few wild mint leaves he'd collected, and settled on the flat rock by the pond. In that quiet, he felt the land breathing—frogs croaked, crickets chirped, water lapped softly against the shore. He pulled out his journal, writing by the flicker of his headlamp:

Made camp in a secret valley pond. Beautiful here—trout in the shallows, a doe at sunset. Reminds me how the forest is infinite in its layers. Tomorrow, I'll climb the ridge and see what's beyond. Tonight, it's me and the stars.

When he finished, he carefully doused the fire, stirred the ashes, and secured his food bag high in a nearby tree. Crawling into his tent, he settled onto his sleeping pad, listening to the night's lullaby until sleep overtook him.

Morning arrived with a soft glow that filtered through the tent's nylon walls. George woke early, drawn by the promise of exploring the ridge above the valley. After a quick breakfast of oatmeal and coffee heated over the rekindled fire, he broke camp, ensuring no trace remained except the faintest impression of a tent. He hoisted his pack, heavier now with slightly damp gear from the night's dew, and started up the slope beyond the pond.

The climb proved steep, requiring him to weave between boulders and use his walking stick for balance. Sweat beaded on his brow, and the forest thickened, offering glimpses of the sun rising between trunks. The calls of birds echoed around him—warblers, thrushes, and the occasional distant drumming of a woodpecker. He pressed on, methodical in his steps, until eventually the forest began to thin. Sunlight grew brighter, and the ground turned rocky underfoot. A final scramble over jagged rocks brought him to the ridge's crest.

There, he emerged into an open vantage that left him breathless. The ridge stretched in a long sweep, partially bald, with stunted pine and low-growing shrubs clinging to cracks in the granite. The sky seemed immense, a brilliant vault of cobalt blue. Below lay the valley he'd left, its pond glinting like a polished coin. Beyond that, rolling hills of green receded into the horizon. Far off, the lake where he lived nestled among countless trees—a sparkle beneath the sun's reflection. A wind, cool and steady, ruffled his beard.

George found a flat rock and removed his pack, letting the breeze dry the sweat from his shirt. He savored the view, feeling a quiet pride at having reached such a spot under his own power. The vantage was a testament to the land's scale: no roads, no signs of human interference beyond distant hints of logging roads. Just wilderness, stretching as far as his eyes could see. For a long time, he sat there in silence, heart stirred by the grandeur of it all.

As he rested, a flicker of motion drew his gaze. Near a clump of blueberries, a lean shape moved. At first, George thought it might be a Coyote, but as it stepped into clearer view, the creature's tawny coat and long tail gave it away—a Puma, sometimes called a Mountain Lion or Cougar. His pulse quickened. These elusive cats were rarely seen in this region, though rumors persisted of their presence. He watched the Puma test the air with its nose, muscles coiled beneath a sleek hide. Even from a distance, George felt the cat's power.

He froze, not wanting to startle or provoke it. The Puma, in turn, seemed unaware of him or, at least, not threatened. It nosed around the bushes, likely searching for small prey or simply passing through. The sunlight glinted off its fur, revealing a tawny mixture of gold and brown. For a solid minute, George dared not breathe. Then, with a sinuous grace, the cat padded across the rocks and out of sight behind the ridge's far slope, leaving behind only faint impressions in the moss.

George let out a slow exhale. His heart pounded as if he'd just run a race. The Puma's presence felt like a rare blessing, a glimpse into the deeper mystery of this wilderness. He realized how fortunate he was to witness such a creature in broad daylight, perched on a ridge far from roads and noise. Gathering himself, he scribbled a quick note in his journal—*Puma on the ridge, morning sun, moved with silent grace.* The day felt charged with significance now, as if the forest had offered him a secret seldom revealed.

With the Puma gone, George rose and explored the ridge more thoroughly. Low shrubs clung to the rocky soil, dotted with ripening blueberries. He picked a handful, popping them into his mouth. Their burst of tart sweetness made him grin. He also spotted stunted conifers leaning in the wind, their trunks twisted by years of storms. The sun climbed higher, intensifying the heat, but the ridge's breeze eased the discomfort.

Eventually, he traced a faint game trail sloping downward. The trail descended toward a chain of small lakes nestled in the valley beyond. Perhaps he'd find a quiet spot to set camp again, or even fish for dinner. Driven by curiosity and the pull of undiscovered country, he followed the path. The terrain led him over scattered boulders, under bent pines, and around tangles of low branches. Occasionally, he had to slide down on hands and knees where the slope grew steep.

Early afternoon found him in a wooded hollow, the air thick with humidity. A small creek meandered through moss-laden stones, and the hush of deeper forest swallowed any trace of the ridge's sweeping views. Here, the atmosphere felt more secretive. Mushrooms sprouted in damp patches, their caps red or brown, shining with moisture. George carefully tested a few logs, sometimes turning one over to reveal scurrying beetles or an occasional salamander. Life abounded in hidden corners.

A faint thunder rumbled overhead. Looking up, George saw the sky had darkened with gathering clouds. Summer storms were frequent visitors, often forming in the heat of the afternoon. The forest canopy disguised much of the threat, but he could sense the electricity in the air. Pressing forward, he aimed to find a suitable campsite before the rain arrived. The promise of a snug shelter in a new location spurred his steps.

The first raindrops splattered the leaves just as George rounded a bend and caught sight of a small lake—no more than a large pond, really—ringed by tall cedars. A narrow beach of coarse sand and pebbles offered enough space to pitch a tent above the waterline. Satisfied, he hurried to set up camp, the sky now throbbing with thunder and the gloom of afternoon turning to near twilight.

The rain intensified, drumming on the tent's rainfly, turning the sandy beach into a patchwork of puddles. George ducked inside, carefully stowing his gear in the vestibule. Flashes of lightning lit the tent in stark white flickers. He felt the wind buffet the walls. Despite the turbulence, he relaxed, listening to nature's fury from a place of relative safety. Rain hammered overhead, and thunder's rumble vibrated the ground beneath him.

He lit a small lantern, deciding to pass the time by revisiting the watercolor kit he'd brought. Splayed out in the tent, with his sleeping pad as a makeshift desk, he painted quick impressions of the ridgeline from memory—a wash of blue and gray for the sky, deep greens for the sweeping forest, and perhaps a suggestion of a tawny shape prowling among the brush. The storm outside lent drama to his brushstrokes. Water dripped from the seam of his tent, reminding him of how small he was in the face of such weather, how the wilderness shaped every plan.

After an hour or so, the thunder receded. The wind calmed, though rain still fell steadily, easing into a steady patter. George realized he was hungry, so he rummaged for a packet of dried stew mix and prepared it with water on his small camp stove, right in the tent's vestibule. Steam rose as he stirred, mingling with the lantern glow. When the stew was done, he savored each bite, warmed from within while outside the forest glistened under the soft hush of ongoing rain.

Darkness arrived early thanks to the thick cloud cover. Once the rain subsided to a drizzle, George stepped out to assess any damage. The lake was calm, reflective in the faint gloom. He could see the silhouettes of cedars and spruces around him, raindrops still clinging to needles. The air felt cool, saturated with the odor of wet earth and pine. Moonlight was hidden behind the clouds, leaving only the ambient glow of a distant lightning flash every now and then.

He walked along the shore, the sand squelching underfoot. The lake, fed by the recent storm, rippled softly. Frogs resumed their croaking, and somewhere a loon called—a haunting cry that seemed to echo across the water. George paused, letting that lonely sound wrap around him. It was the voice of the wilderness, timeless and plaintive, a reminder of how these animals thrived without human interference.

Back at his tent, he stashed his food once more, mindful of bears lured by the smell of dinner scraps. Then, crawling into his sleeping bag, he let the day's images flood his mind: the doe by the pond, the Puma on the ridge, the hush of the cedar-lined lake in the storm's aftermath. He thought also of the promise of tomorrow. He might explore further, or perhaps loop back a different route to see new corners of the forest. Sleep came easily, the patter of rain providing a gentle lullaby against the taut fabric of the tent.

Sometime before sunrise, George stirred. The rain had stopped, leaving the forest dripping and hushed. Pale light crept through the tent walls. He unzipped the flap to find a world renewed. Mist floated over the small lake, swirling among the cedar trunks in shifting veils. The ground glistened, each leaf holding a bead of water that refracted the faint dawn glow. He boiled water for coffee, sipping the dark liquid while seated on a fallen log near the shore, letting the morning's stillness fill him.

He mulled over whether to linger another day, but a tug in his heart pointed him homeward. He'd seen wondrous sights on this journey, and though the wilderness beckoned endlessly, he felt a pull to return to his cabin by nightfall. He decided to chart a looping path that would eventually lead back to the lake he knew so well. With that in mind, he broke camp, carefully dispersing the stones he'd used to anchor his tent, leaving no trace. The forest would heal any footprints soon enough. A final glance at the tranquil lake—and he set off.

The path out was faint and meandering, but he followed the lay of the land, guided by occasional blazes or the subtle hints in terrain. At times, he had to forge his own route, stepping through ferns that brushed his legs and cause beads of water to cascade down his boots. The forest was alive with birds greeting the morning sun: a Gray Jay perched overhead, uttering a raspy note, while a thrush's flute-like song resounded from deeper shadows. He walked steadily, pausing now and then to relish a new perspective—perhaps a hidden glen or a meandering creek.

By midmorning, the clouds began to thin, allowing the sun to burn through. Gradually, the forest transitioned back to more familiar territory. He recognized a certain rock formation, then a gentle slope descending into the broader valley that led toward his home lake. The comforting sense of returning encompassed him. Hours passed in peaceful strides until, finally, the distant sparkle of the lake's waters appeared through the trees.

Late in the day, George emerged onto the very trail he had left just two dawns before. The sight of the main lake felt both homely and grand. The sun hung low, gilding the ripples with amber light. He made his way around the shore, approaching the place where he'd first set off. His legs ached pleasantly, and his spirit hummed with fulfillment. The cabin came into view, smoke gently curling from the chimney—he realized with a start that he'd left no fire behind, so it must be the last remnants of his stove's banked embers or some illusions of warm air in the evening light. Regardless, it felt like a reassuring welcome.

He stepped onto his porch, removing his boots and setting them aside. The clearing around the cabin was quiet except for the drone of insects and the lapping of water. Letting out a long breath, he placed his pack by the door. Already, his mind buzzed with memories of the trip: the secluded pond, the Puma's silent crossing, the storm by the cedar-lined lake. He would carry these experiences in his heart, weaving them into the tapestry of his life here. Perhaps he'd paint scenes from the ridge, or develop the sketch of that cat's sleek body, or simply let the memories nestle in his journal.

Inside, the cabin smelled familiar—woodsmoke, pine logs, and faint traces of the last meal he'd cooked. He lit a lamp, the warm glow chasing away the encroaching dusk. Stripping off his pack, he sighed as the weight left his shoulders. He'd re-stock, re-supply, and plan the next excursion soon enough. For now, he craved a quick wash and a simple dinner. He heated water on the stove, splashing the warmth over his arms, face, and neck. The sensation of cleanliness mingled with the lingering fatigue in his muscles, a pleasant ache that testified to miles walked and ridges climbed.

For dinner, he fried a few potatoes from his garden and added fresh onions, filling the cabin with a homey aroma. As he ate, he reflected on how connected he felt to the land—sleeping under the stars, waking with the sun, following the whims of weather, and discovering creatures that roamed where roads did not exist. The forest had once again reminded him of its vastness, its mysteries, and its capacity to offer solace for a heart seeking contact with deeper rhythms.

After cleaning up, he settled in his rocking chair by the window. The sky outside shimmered with the last vestiges of daylight—pink and orange ribbons fading into purple. Across the lake, a loon's tremolo cry echoed, as if welcoming him back. He opened his journal to a fresh page and began writing in careful script:

Home again after two nights in the high country. Found a secluded valley with a pond—met a doe at twilight. Saw a Puma on the ridge (rare, silent grace). Storm rolled in by the next lake, but the tent held firm. This land reveals itself layer by layer, each step unveiling new wonders. Tired, but grateful.

He paused, listening to the forest's hush. He scribbled a quick pencil sketch of the Puma, capturing the slope of its back and the proud set of its head. Then he added details of the ridgeline—gnarled pines, broad vistas, the swirl of clouds. His hand lingered on the page, remembering. The day's warmth still clung to the cabin, even as a gentle breeze slipped through the open window, ruffling the edges of the map on the table.

Eventually, he closed the journal. Outside, the stars emerged, twinkling over the vast expanse of woods and water. He glanced at the silent map, still spread where he'd left it. So many routes and unnamed glens remained. Perhaps next time, he'd venture further east, or follow that intriguing creek he'd noticed on the ridge. The possibilities fanned out before him like the starry sky, each trail a promise of discovery.

He doused the lantern, letting the moon's silver light wash the cabin in soft shadows. In the hearth's glow—he'd lit a small, low fire for ambiance—he noted how his boots, caked with mud and pine needles, sat quietly near the door. Tomorrow, he'd clean and oil them, gather fresh produce from the garden, and return to his daily rhythms. But the memory of these last two nights, spent amid hidden ponds and rocky overlooks, would linger in his mind, fueling daydreams and gentle contentment for weeks to come.

Stretching, he climbed into his bunk, the day's exertion making every muscle sigh. The hush of the woods folded around him, and a faint call of a Barred Owl drifted over the lake. He let his eyelids grow heavy, lulled by that comforting presence of wildness outside. Just before sleep claimed him, a final image rose in his mind: the Puma on the ridge, outlined against the endless sky, as if it watched over these forests with ancient, knowing eyes. With that vision, George embraced the quiet and allowed the forest's lullaby to guide him into deep, untroubled dreams.

In the morning, he would wake at home, the old cabin standing firm on the lake's edge. Yet he'd carry within him the hush of the hidden valley, the memory of storms on a distant shore, and the silhouette of a cat that prowled the ridgeline. This was life in the woods—a steady cycle of homecomings, wanderings, and the silent revelations that nature offered the patient traveler.

183

10

A PUMA'S PRESENCE

A few weeks after returning from his camping trip a gentle warmth clung to the late summer air when George first caught sight of new animal tracks. He had set out at daybreak, as was his habit, hoping to gather fresh photographs of the forest in the soft morning light. The sun, still low on the horizon, cast long shadows across the ferns and pine needles, and a light mist hovered over the lake's surface. Beneath his sturdy boots, the ground felt springy—a mixture of pine mulch and damp earth that had soaked up the recent rains. Dressed in his usual hiking attire (an old flannel over a thin shirt and well-worn canvas trousers), George felt that quiet thrill of possibility that always accompanied an early start in the woods.

He was climbing a gentle slope near a stand of birch trees when he spotted them—footprints unlike those of a deer, bear, or wolf. They were large and round, the imprint showing four toes plus a faint suggestion of a heel pad. The shape was too big to be a bobcat's. He crouched slowly, leaning his walking stick against a birch trunk and inspecting the tracks. The crisp outline and the size reminded him of the Puma tracks he'd seen once before, years ago. Or, more recently, the fleeting glimpse he'd caught of a Puma during one of his backpacking treks through the ridge country (the memory still fresh from a few weeks prior). But this time, these tracks were closer to his cabin—much closer than he'd ever expected.

A ripple of excitement and caution shot through him. Pumas, or cougars, remained elusive in these parts. Although legends and occasional sightings circulated among the locals, actual encounters were rare. Even the wildlife rangers seldom confirmed their presence, though they suspected a few might roam the deep northern woods. But here was evidence, pressed into the damp earth—tangible proof that at least one Puma moved through the forest not far from George's home.

He paused to run his fingertips around the edges of the print. Still soft, edges crisp, so they hadn't been made too long ago—maybe last night or in the earliest hours before dawn. The hair on the back of his neck prickled at the thought of a large, powerful cat gliding through the darkness while he slept soundly in his cabin. Yet alongside any fear, George felt awe and respect. This was a reminder that, despite his years living in these woods, the land still held mysteries far beyond his domain.

He took a few photos of the tracks with his camera, stepping carefully so as not to disturb them too much. Then he rose, scanning the surrounding undergrowth. Morning light flickered through birch leaves, playing across the mossy ground. No sign of the Puma itself, only the silent statement of its footprints. Feeling a renewed attentiveness, George continued on his way, each step more measured than before. His original plan had been to loop around the western shore of the lake for scenic photos, but now he decided to adjust his route, following the direction of the tracks for a short stretch. Curiosity pulled him forward, though he reminded himself not to be reckless.

For half an hour, George traced faint signs through the forest. In addition to a few more partial paw prints in muddy patches, he spotted a bent fern here, a scattering of pine needles there—small clues that might have been left by any passing animal, but that he tentatively connected to the Puma's route. The trail veered away from the lake, weaving between stands of cedar and pine. A hush hung over the woods, broken only by the occasional call of a Jay or the scolding chatter of a red squirrel. George's senses felt heightened; every shift of foliage or snap of a twig drew his attention.

Eventually, the tracks disappeared into rocky ground near a shallow ravine. George found no more impressions, though he combed the area thoroughly. He considered venturing down the ravine, where a small creek sometimes flowed. But the morning's prime light was fading, and he recalled that he'd only planned a short outing. He still wanted to get back to the cabin for lunch, and besides, it wasn't wise to push too far after a big cat alone. So, he turned back, all the while scanning the tree line in case the Puma might be watching from a hidden vantage. The notion sent a pleasant chill through him, that old tingle of being in an apex predator's realm.

The walk home was uneventful. Mossy logs, scattered mushrooms, and a few glimpses of chipmunks rummaging in the leaf litter reminded him that most forest life went on, oblivious to one man's curiosity about a single predator. Around mid-morning, he crested a small rise and caught sight of the lake. Sunlight glinted off the water, a playful sparkle that made him squint. The horizon promised a clear afternoon. Perhaps he'd do some painting later, or maybe cast a line to see if the bass were biting. But first, he wanted to jot down this morning's finding in his journal.

Back home, George placed his camera on the table and brewed a fresh pot of coffee. While he waited for the percolator to do its gentle dance on the stovetop, he flipped open his leather-bound journal. The pages rustled, already heavy with sketches, notes, and reflections from the past months—fishing successes, descriptions of spring blossoms, that time he encountered a mother black bear rummaging near the woodpile. Now, he devoted a fresh page to the Puma tracks.

August 2nd, early morning. Found large cat prints near the birch stand north of the cabin. Likely Puma. Tracks were fresh, edges well-defined. Followed them for half a mile before losing them in rocky terrain. No direct sighting, but thrilling to confirm its presence so close by.

He added a rough sketch of one paw print, approximating its size based on his memory. Then he poured himself a mug of coffee, savoring the aroma that filled the cabin. Outside, bees hummed around the wildflowers along his porch, and a Red Squirrel scurried across the roof. The day's temperature promised to climb, but the interior of the cabin remained cool, thanks to the logs' insulation.

As he sipped, he mused about how to proceed. He wasn't bent on chasing the Puma or intruding upon its territory. But he did want to remain vigilant and maybe glean a better understanding of its habits. He decided that over the next few days, he'd keep an eye out for fresh signs, perhaps set up his trail camera (which he usually used for capturing deer and bear footage) in a strategic spot. If the cat continued to roam the area, a camera might confirm its route or even yield a photo. The thought excited him. Despite living a solitary life, George felt a fondness for documenting the wildlife that shared these woods, as if forging a silent camaraderie with them.

After lunch—a simple sandwich with vegetables from his garden—George loaded his canoe with fishing tackle, painting supplies, and a small folding chair. Summer's sun hovered high, hot and bright, and a gentle breeze stirred the lake's surface. He dipped a hand in the water as he pushed off from shore, finding it pleasantly cool. For a while, he paddled along the shoreline, pausing now and then to cast a line for bass or to anchor and do a quick plein air study of the lake's mid-summer greens. He caught a couple of modest smallmouths, releasing them after a brief tussle. The fishing wasn't spectacular, but the day's serenity more than made up for that.

Across the water, the forest sloped upward, a tapestry of birch, poplar, pine, and spruce. He thought about the Puma again—where it might be at that moment, if it ever slunk down to the lake's edge to drink or ambush prey. A large cat could remain unseen for weeks, even near a human dwelling, so adept were they at moving silently. He felt a pang of humility: humans often believed themselves masters of the land, yet a single Puma could roam these woods, intangible as a ghost, answering only to its own instincts and the ancient laws of survival.

In the late afternoon, he found a shady spot near some tall reeds, propped the canoe, and set up his easel on a little patch of rocky shore. He worked on a small painting of the water's reflection, capturing how the late-summer sun tinted the ripples with gold. Dragonflies buzzed around him, occasionally landing on the tip of his rod or the edge of his canvas. Their iridescent wings flashed in the sunlight. Each brushstroke carried the joy of being immersed in nature's gentle flux, an echo of the day's unexpected encounter with the tracks. He felt energized, painting swiftly yet mindfully, letting the bright palette reflect the warmth of August.

Evening approached before he realized how long he'd been at it. With a soft sigh, he packed up and paddled back home. As he secured the canoe onshore, he saw a few fish jump in the fading light, their splashes sending rings across the placid water. The forest's hush deepened, cicadas droning in the canopy. He ate a quick supper of grilled vegetables, then settled onto his porch with a cup of tea. The sky turned a wash of pink and orange, and the first stars peeked through. Thoughts of the Puma lingered in the back of his mind, nudging him to set out that trail camera as soon as possible. Tomorrow, he resolved, would be the day.

Early the next morning, George rummaged in his storage chest until he found the trail camera he'd purchased a few years back. It was a simple model, triggered by motion, able to capture low-light images. Usually, he set it up in autumn to watch deer or occasional black bear activity around the orchard near town. This time, he'd aim it at the area where he'd discovered the Puma tracks. Once his coffee was drained, he tucked the camera into a sling bag, grabbed a handful of small bungee cords, and slung his daypack with snacks and water over his shoulder.

The sun had barely cleared the treetops when he headed out, returning to the same birch stand. The tracks had dried somewhat, but the impression remained, albeit fainter. He walked carefully, scanning for any new prints or signs of disturbance. Nothing fresh caught his eye, though. Finding a vantage that covered a likely path, he chose a sturdy pine trunk for the camera. From there, it overlooked a faint game trail winding toward the ravine. If the Puma returned, or if any large creature passed through, the lens would catch it.

Securing the camera with bungee cords, he tested the motion sensor, making sure it had a clear line of sight. Then he set the date and time stamp. With that done, he felt a small thrill—like a child waiting for a surprise. Now it was a matter of patience and luck. The Puma might never come back this way, or it could pass by in the dead of night. Either outcome was part of the forest's unpredictable nature.

On his return trip, George decided to meander along a different route, hoping to skirt near a patch of wild berries he knew thrived this time of year. Indeed, the brambles were heavy with plump, dark raspberries. He picked a small bagful, occasionally popping a sweet berry into his mouth. The tang of fresh fruit gave him a sense of summer's bounty, a reminder that while he watched for predators, the forest offered nourishment in countless forms.

The days that followed passed in a comfortable routine. George tended his garden, fished in the mornings, and resumed painting sessions during the afternoons. He'd made no new Puma discoveries—no fresh tracks, no glimpses. Yet the knowledge that such a creature might be roaming the vicinity lent an extra thrill to his daily wanderings. At times, he caught himself glancing over his shoulder if he heard a rustle, or pausing to let his eyes adjust when stepping from bright sunlight into shadowed clearings.

About a week after setting up the camera, he decided to check on it. The morning was cool, a hint of autumn's approach in the breeze, though summer's warmth still dominated the daytime hours. With his daypack lightly stocked—water, a few snacks, and an empty memory card—he set out for the birch stand. The forest welcomed him with a hush, dappled light dancing on the path. Jays squawked in the distance, and occasionally a woodpecker's drumming broke the morning calm.

He reached the pine tree and found the camera intact. Eagerly, he unstrapped it, powered it off, and swapped the memory card. Before heading back, he considered checking the ravine. The air felt still, the leaves hardly moving. Why not, he thought, just a quick look to see if any tracks turned up along the water's edge. Perhaps he'd find more sign of the Puma. If not, the walk would still be pleasant.

He descended the rocky slope carefully, each step tested for traction. The ravine's narrow creek trickled faintly, its volume reduced by August's dryness. Clumps of moss covered stones, and ferns drooped in the mild heat. Around a bend, he froze—a shape moved near the creek bank. For an instant, time seemed to slow. There, crouched in the shade, was the Puma.

It was bigger than he'd anticipated, muscles rippling under a tawny coat. The cat had been drinking at the creek, silent and unaware of George's approach. But now, sensing him, it lifted its head, ears pricked. Bright amber eyes locked on George's figure. His heart pounded like a drum. He stood motionless, hardly breathing. The Puma's gaze was intense but not overtly hostile—more surprised. They stared at each other across maybe thirty yards of rocky streambed.

George's mind raced, recalling every piece of advice for wildlife encounters: stand tall, don't run, appear calm. With painstaking care, he kept his posture upright, not wanting to appear threatening or skittish. The Puma sniffed the air, a low rumble in its throat—perhaps a warning or a statement of presence. George's pulse hammered. He slid one foot back, testing the ground for a stable step in case he needed to retreat. The cat's eyes narrowed, flicking to that motion. Another quiet rumble, not quite a growl. It stepped sideways, giving itself room.

For a second that felt eternal, they regarded each other in the hush of the ravine. George whispered a gentle greeting, as if acknowledging the Puma's dominion. The cat's tail twitched. Then, with a fluid turn, it loped up the opposite slope, silent as a phantom. In seconds, it vanished into the undergrowth. The forest echoed with the aftermath, as though exhaling a breath collectively held.

George remained rooted, heart pounding. Gradually, he let out a shaky breath. That fleeting exchange had been both terrifying and extraordinary. He rubbed sweaty palms on his trousers, thankful that the Puma had chosen to depart rather than challenge him. Slowly, he backed away, eyes scanning the ravine's crest. No sign of the cat. He made his way back toward the pine where the camera had been, knees feeling suddenly weak. Once back on level ground, he sat on a fallen log to let his nerves settle.

Back at the cabin an hour later, George realized his mouth was still dry. He brewed tea, sipping it while replaying the encounter in his mind. The cat's silent presence, the unwavering stare—it confirmed everything he admired and respected about apex predators. They needed no permission to exist in these woods; the land was theirs as much as it was his. That truth never felt so immediate as when he locked eyes with the Puma.

He powered on his computer (an old laptop he rarely used except for checking trail camera footage or storing photos) and inserted the memory card from the camera. His hands still trembled with residual adrenaline. The camera's files began to load. Flicking through images, he saw a handful of nighttime deer, a raccoon waddling across the frame, and then—there it was. A series of shots showing the Puma strolling past at night, eyes glowing in the infrared flash. Its silhouette looked strong, the tail long, the body lean. Another shot caught it mid-step, muscles flexing. George felt his breath catch. Proof, at last, that the big cat truly frequented these woods.

The timestamps indicated the Puma passed the camera on multiple nights, typically between midnight and the pre-dawn hours. George scrolled until he found a surprise: a mother black bear and two cubs crossing the same path a few days later. The forest was busier than he sometimes realized! He saved the photos, printing a few to tack onto his "wildlife sightings" corkboard by the cabin's entryway. He suspected only a handful of people in the region would believe these Puma pictures, but that didn't matter to him. The forest had spoken, and he was merely an observer taking notes.

In the weeks that followed, George maintained a more careful routine. He continued fishing, painting, and gardening, but always remained mindful of the Puma's potential proximity. He changed up his usual routes to check the trail camera, sometimes bringing along his old bear spray as a precaution (even if cougars and bears rarely crossed paths with humans unless provoked). A sense of thrilling respect coursed through him each time he wandered near the ravine. He half-hoped to glimpse the Puma again, but reasoned it was likely a once-in-a-lifetime brush with wild grace. Some nights, as he sat by the fireplace tying new flies for the upcoming autumn trout run, he wondered if the Puma passed silently through the moonlit forest outside his cabin, searching for deer or traveling to distant ridges.

He recorded each new camera capture in his journal. The Puma appeared sporadically—no set pattern, sometimes skipping a week or more, then returning on consecutive nights. George guessed it had a wide territory, possibly crossing multiple drainage basins. Summer was prime hunting season for a large cat, with plenty of deer, small mammals, and even the occasional porcupine if it was daring enough. Meanwhile, the mother black bear with cubs also showed up sporadically. Wolf howls echoed once or twice in the distance, though George hadn't glimpsed them in a while. The forest felt alive with predators, a testament to its healthy ecosystem.

On nights when the moon was bright, George often strolled to the edge of the lake, letting silver light guide his steps. If the wind was calm, he'd watch for shapes drifting near the shoreline, or reflections of eyes glinting in the dark. He never saw the Puma there—likely it preferred the deeper woods—but these nightly walks satisfied his longing to remain connected to the wilderness. He'd stand on the lake bank, listening to loon calls, breathing the pine-scented air. Then, satisfied, he'd return to the safety of his cabin, aware that something larger might roam beyond the flicker of his lantern.

A few days later, George noticed a shift in the air—the subtle turning toward autumn. Mornings carried a crispness, and leaves at the forest's edges hinted at yellow. One evening, he arrived home from a late fishing trip under a sky streaked with crimson clouds. As he approached the porch, he froze. There, on the ground, lay a freshly killed rabbit, untouched except for a single bite near its neck. No signs of a struggle. No tracks in the dusty patch that he could discern immediately, but suspicion flared. Could this be the work of the Puma?

He surveyed the scene carefully, backtracking into the yard. A sense of unease mixed with wonder. Why would the cat leave a kill so near the cabin? Predatory animals rarely wasted food, and cougars especially tended to drag prey into cover for feeding. The rabbit looked almost staged. George knelt to inspect it—still warm, no evidence of feeding. A chilled ripple went through him. Animals sometimes abandoned a kill if startled, but it was odd for a Puma to drop prey so close to human habitation. A coyote or fox might have done so as well, but the marks on the rabbit's neck suggested a powerful jaw, more in line with a cougar's or a large canine.

George stood, scanning the twilight. Nothing moved in the clearing or among the pines. Quiet as a held breath. He decided to dispose of the carcass quickly, burying it a short distance from the cabin to avoid attracting other scavengers. At the same time, he wondered about the significance—if any existed beyond random chance. A part of him recalled stories of big cats occasionally "gifting" or caching prey when they felt no immediate hunger. It could be the Puma had been startled by something, dropping the rabbit. Or was it a gesture of some primal recognition? He smiled wryly at the notion, unsure whether to chalk it up to superstition or a remarkable coincidence.

That night, he lit a lantern and read for a while, but his thoughts drifted repeatedly to the rabbit. In all his years here, no predator had left fresh prey on his doorstep. The idea of a large cat frequenting his property was thrilling but also sobering. He triple-checked that his doors were latched and windows secured, not out of real fear but out of caution. Before bed, he scrawled a note in his journal:

August 8th: Found a fresh-killed rabbit by the porch at dusk. Bite marks suggest a powerful predator—Puma or large coyote? Strange to abandon it so close to my cabin. No sign of a struggle. Maybe the cat was startled. Feels like a quiet message from the forest.

As September loomed, the forest's mood began shifting from summer's fullness to autumn's anticipation. The days remained warm, but the nights cooled more quickly, and hints of color touched the underbrush. George continued to keep an eye on his trail camera, capturing sporadic images of the Puma. Each time, the cat looked healthy and strong, sometimes strolling along, other times moving at a swift pace. Once, the camera caught it with a rabbit dangling from its jaws. Perhaps the same type of rabbit left by his porch, though that remained guesswork.

His daily life carried on, quietly enriched by the knowledge that a rare and regal predator roamed the same woods he called home. He talked about it only once or twice in town, though people mostly waved off the idea—"Plenty of folks claim cougars are out there, but I haven't seen one in decades," they'd say. George simply smiled, content to keep the Puma's presence to himself, aside from the few photos pinned to his cabin's corkboard.

One evening, as the sun dipped behind the tallest pines, he took his canoe out for a leisurely paddle. The sky blazed orange and pink, reflecting on the water's surface in brilliant hues. He glided toward the far shore, fishing rod left behind in favor of simple enjoyment. In the hush, he recalled how many wonders this land had offered him: Moose encounters, black bears rummaging, a fleeting Puma on a hidden ridge, fresh rabbit tracks across the winter snow, loons calling at twilight. He'd lived many seasons here, yet each day felt like a promise of something new.

Reaching a small inlet, he rested his paddle and let the canoe drift. Shadows stretched across the lake, and the first stars twinkled overhead. A loon's tremolo echoed, then fell silent. The forest loomed around him, a dark silhouette. He thought of the Puma pacing somewhere in the night, agile and free. One day, it might wander on. Or perhaps it would remain, raising cubs if it were female, establishing a territory in the hidden hollows of the north woods. The unknown possibility excited him.

Before the last of the light faded, George guided his canoe back toward his cabin. Flickers of warm lamplight spilled through the window, a beacon calling him home. He pulled the canoe ashore, secured it, and made his way inside. The cabin embraced him with the comforting scents of old wood and a faint memory of the stew he'd cooked earlier. He poured a mug of tea and stood by the open window, letting the night air brush his face.

A gentle sense of awe settled on him, reminiscent of the hush that followed his meeting with the Puma in the ravine. So much of the natural world remained beyond words, beyond rational explanation—an endless, beautiful dance of predator and prey, growth and decay, presence and absence. To be a small part of it, to bear witness, felt like a gift.

In that quiet moment, he resolved to keep living in harmony with the forest's deeper rhythms, mindful of the shadows that moved beyond the circle of his lantern's light. The Puma, wherever it roamed tonight, represented a final frontier of wilderness—untamed, majestic, and ephemeral. Let it remain so, George thought. Let it keep the world mysterious, teaching those who dwell here that life's greatest treasures often lie just beyond our comfortable reach.

He blew out the lamp, the cabin plunging into darkness except for moonlight from the window. On the table, his journal lay open, the latest entry describing the trail camera photos. Tomorrow, he might add another note about the day's reflections, or perhaps a new surprise would greet him. For now, he slipped into bed, the woods humming with nocturnal life. The presence of a Puma in these parts felt like an ancient secret whispered from the treetops. George let that secret lull him to sleep, a contented smile curving under his thick gray beard.

And so, the hush of the day settled around the cabin—a hush touched by the silent footsteps of a

Puma that roamed through George's domain, linking his ordinary life with the timeless spirit of the untamed forest.

11

SUMMER'S PEAK

A low hum of cicadas met George as he stepped off his porch into the full embrace of a midsummer morning. Heat shimmered in the air, softening the forest's edges and giving the clearing a hazy glow. For days, the temperatures had climbed steadily, the sun lingering high and strong, baking the roof shingles of the cabin and coaxing sweet resin from the pines. Clouds drifted sparsely overhead, offering little promise of relief. It was the season's high point— long hours of daylight and warm nights, the forest so deeply green it felt almost impenetrable.

George paused to relish the morning. He wore a light, short-sleeved shirt beneath his old suspenders, having abandoned flannel weeks ago. Gazing around the clearing, he noted how tall the grasses had grown, seeded by the warm summer rains of July. Beyond them, the lake glittered under a sky of clear, cerulean blue. A loon's distant cry echoed. This hush, woven of insect buzz and soft water sounds, gave the day a languid, almost drowsy rhythm. Summer was at its peak, pressing the forest into vibrant fullness.

Yet beneath the calm, George felt a small tremor of excitement. Today he planned a trip into the nearby town for a community event that happened once each summer: the Kincaid Falls Heritage Fair. He hadn't gone the previous year—winter stores had held out, and he'd chosen solitude over socializing. But this time, Linda from the café had mentioned it warmly during his last visit, reminding him of the homemade pies, local crafts, and a chance to meet new folks. After a moment's hesitation, he'd promised to attend. Part of him relished the thought of stepping briefly into a swirl of neighborly bustle before retreating to his cabin once more.

Stowing a few supplies in the back of his old pickup truck, George checked his fuel levels, then took a moment to top off the oil. The engine sputtered, coughed, then roared to life—a stubborn old friend that seemed determined to keep running as long as George treated it right. He placed a small cooler of water and iced tea on the passenger seat. The day would be scorching; he could practically feel the heat radiating off the truck's metal. With a final glance at his cabin to ensure the door was firmly latched, he set off down the rutted dirt path toward the main road.

The first leg of the drive meandered through dense stands of birch and poplar, their pale trunks flickering in the sun. Splashes of green ferns covered the understory, and every so often, a deer would lift its head from feeding to watch him pass. The road eventually shifted from gravel to cracked asphalt, glimmering in the hot sunlight. As he neared town, he noticed lines of corn in tidy fields, the tall stalks brushing the sky, and patches of wildflowers dancing at the edges of farmland. There were more vehicles, too—some pulling trailers loaded with livestock or covered with fair displays. The small community of Kincaid Falls stirred, everyone bustling toward the same destination.

Soon, the humble welcome sign for Kincaid Falls came into view, its paint chipped but still cheery. The single blinking traffic light at the town's main intersection guided George in. He turned onto the side road leading toward the fairgrounds, which in truth was nothing more than a large, grassy field behind the school. Parking attendants in fluorescent vests waved him into a spot near a stand of oak trees where the shade relieved some of the sun's intensity. Killing the engine, he slipped out, dusted off his hat, and surveyed the scene.

Already, the fair was in full swing. Rows of colorful booths stretched across the open field: homemade jams and jellies, baked goods, crafts, and local produce arranged in neat displays. The air carried an enticing mix of grilled meats, sweet cotton candy, and fresh hay. Children dashed about, chasing each other through the grass, while their parents chatted with neighbors or examined the wares. A small band played fiddles and guitars on a makeshift stage, tunes dancing on the warm breeze.

George wandered through slowly, tipping his hat in polite greeting to those who recognized him as "the man from the lake." A few folks approached to ask how he'd been, remark on the weather, or inquire about the fishing. He answered with his customary gentleness, offering small smiles and the occasional anecdote about summer's fish activity or the raccoons that prowled near his cabin at night.

As he strolled between booths, an older woman selling jars of pickles waved him over. Her sign read: *Brenda's Famous Dill Pickles and More.* She insisted he sample a spear of tangy dill, which he accepted with gratitude, enjoying the crisp, briny taste that cut through the day's heat. Further along, a man in a broad straw hat was hawking local honey. George bought a jar—his supply at the cabin had dwindled, and he preferred the robust flavor of raw, unfiltered honey from these hives. The man beamed as he dropped the jar into a small paper bag.

The band's tune shifted into a lively reel, the fiddles rising over the chatter. Children squealed with laughter, and a faint whiff of sawdust from some woodcarving demonstration carried on the air. All around, the sense of conviviality was palpable. Though George's heart belonged to the solitude of the woods, he felt a warm stirring of appreciation for this communal spirit. It reminded him that even in a remote region, people found reasons to gather, celebrate, and share in each other's harvests and crafts.

Near the center of the fairgrounds, a row of food stalls offered various treats. George spotted Linda from the café, bustling behind a table laden with pies, sandwiches, and lemonade. Her apron—adorned with daisies—flapped in the breeze as she served a steady line of hungry patrons. Sensing his approach, she looked up, her face lighting with a wide grin.

"Well, if it isn't George!" she called over the general din. "I was starting to worry you wouldn't make it."

"I promised you I'd come," George replied, tipping his hat. "Couldn't pass up your pie on a day like this."

She handed him a slice of strawberry-rhubarb and a cup of cold lemonade, waving away his offer of payment. "On the house—for making good on your promise." Then, quieter, she leaned in. "So how's life up at your cabin? Still having those run-ins with the local wildlife?"

A small smile tugged at his beard. "Oh, plenty. Black bears sniffing around, foxes by the shoreline, and... well, there's a rumor of a big cat."

Linda's eyes widened, but a rush of customers behind George kept her from asking more. "We'll talk later," she said, patting his arm and darting off to fill more orders.

George found a shady patch beneath a cluster of maples where a few hay bales had been arranged as seats. He settled onto one, balancing his lemonade and pie. The sweet-tangy filling burst with flavor—Linda's pies were famous in these parts, and for good reason. He savored each bite, letting the day's heat dissipate in the shade. People ambled by, greeting each other with waves, sometimes giving George a friendly nod. He realized how seldom he saw so many faces at once anymore, and how, in small doses, it felt pleasant to reconnect.

After finishing his slice, George wandered further. A booth displaying hand-carved wooden bowls and spoons caught his eye. Tim, the hardware store owner, was there, skillfully demonstrating how to shape a block of cedar into a spoon. Shavings curled off his carving knife as onlookers leaned in, entranced.

"George!" Tim called, pausing his demonstration. "Glad you came. Need any new lines for that fly reel? Or are you strictly browsing crafts today?"

George chuckled. "Strictly browsing, Tim. How's business?"

Tim shrugged, setting down the knife. "Fair enough for a small town. Summers help keep us afloat—lots of folks repairing cabins, building docks. Speaking of which, you better watch out. I've got my eye on that old canoe of yours. Might trade you a brand-new one for your vintage piece."

George returned a playful grin. "Mine's got character, Tim. I'd never part with it."

They swapped stories about summer repairs and fishing luck. Tim teased George about always coming to town "only when the moon is full," and George retorted that the forest kept him too busy to track the moon's cycles precisely. All in good humor. Then Tim turned back to entertaining the crowd, carving deftly while explaining wood grain and finishing techniques.

George moved on, drifting toward a booth full of colorful quilts. Nearby, a group of elders sat on wooden chairs, fanning themselves with pamphlets about local history. The swirl of conversation, children's laughter, and the melody of the fiddles created a tapestry of warmth and shared living. Though he'd chosen a solitary path years ago, George felt a pang of affection for these neighbors who carried on their own rhythms in Kincaid Falls.

He paused at a small display featuring old photographs of the region: black-and-white pictures of logging camps, men in suspenders hauling massive pines, the early days of the railway. A gray-haired woman in a straw hat gestured at the images, explaining to a group that her grandfather had been among those loggers, clearing land around the lake. George listened quietly, gleaning tidbits of local lore. One photo showed a general store from the 1920s, a rickety building that predated the current one by decades. Another showed the lake from a vantage near where

George's cabin now stood—though in that photo, no structures blemished the shore.

An older man nearby, leaning on a cane, noticed George's interest. "Quite a history we got here, huh?" he said in a raspy voice. "I hear you live up near the big pines?"

George nodded. "Yes, not far from them at all. The cabin's been around a good while, though not as long as these old photos would suggest."

The man introduced himself as Clyde, explaining that he'd grown up in Kincaid Falls, then moved away for work, only to return decades later. His father had told stories about traveling by sled on the lake in winter, bringing goods to remote trappers.

"I bet you're the first real hermit we've had in years," Clyde joked. "How do you fare out there in the deep snows?"

George chuckled softly. "I manage well enough. Lots of firewood, a sturdy cabin. The old folks who built it must have known what they were doing—stays warm even in the worst winter storms."

Clyde nodded, clearly pleased. "Good. Glad to see someone carrying on that tradition of living by the land. Ain't many left who do."

They chatted a bit longer, comparing the area's past and present. Eventually, Clyde spotted someone he recognized and shuffled off, waving goodbye. George lingered, absorbing the images of people who'd walked these forests long before him. The continuity comforted him, bridging the distance between his solitary life and the town's shared heritage.

Before he realized it, the day wore on, shadows beginning to stretch across the fairgrounds. The crowd thickened around suppertime, with more families arriving for the evening's festivities—traditional dancing, local bands, and fireworks rumored at dusk. George meandered past a small pen of goats and chickens, likely part of a children's petting zoo. A few kids squealed with delight, chasing a goat that nibbled at their pockets for treats.

Occasionally, someone recognized George as the "old fisherman from the lake" or "that painter fellow." They asked polite questions about how he'd been, if he'd sold any paintings, whether he needed help winterizing. While he appreciated the concern, he rarely needed assistance—his self-reliance spanned decades. Still, the warmth behind their offers touched him. He realized these people saw him as part of their tapestry, however distant.

That sense of belonging, even in small measure, felt quietly reassuring.

In a corner of the fairgrounds, a makeshift stage awaited for the evening's band performance. Straw bales had been arranged into seats, and a temporary wooden dance floor beckoned. Linda found him there, peeking around for a place to sit. She led him to a bench up front, handing him an extra cup of lemonade. The two chatted amid the swirl of dancers warming up.

"So, about that big cat you mentioned..." Linda teased, eyes sparkling. "I've heard rumors from a few hunters. You actually seen it?"

George hesitated, thinking how to phrase it. "Yes, at least once up close. Found tracks near my cabin a few weeks back, then glimpsed it by a creek. Large. Magnificent."

Linda's jaw dropped slightly. "And you're still out there, unafraid? I'd be terrified."

He shrugged, smile tugging at his beard. "It's no more dangerous than a black bear or wolves—just cautious. I respect its space; it respects mine."

Linda shook her head in mild disbelief. "You're braver than me. If it shows up in town, though, you might be stuck with a whole posse of self-appointed hunters."

George sighed, thinking of how quickly fear could spread among those unaccustomed to large predators. "Hope that never happens. It belongs in the deep woods."

Their conversation faded as the band began tuning—fiddles, banjos, a stand-up bass. Soon, lively music erupted, and dancers took to the wooden floor, stepping in a jovial square dance. Linda drifted off to serve at her stall again, leaving George to watch the swirl of colors and smiling faces. The music was infectious, and he couldn't help tapping his foot. The glow of strings of festival lights against the encroaching twilight created a festive ambiance that felt worlds away from the hush of pines around his cabin.

As dusk settled, the temperature mercifully dropped. The summer heat softened into a balmy warmth, and a gentle breeze carried the tang of grilled food. Some couples switched from square dancing to two-step waltzes. Others lined up for a final round of funnel cakes or homemade ice cream. George found himself drawn toward the edge of the crowd, seeking a quieter nook.

Just then, Burt—the older fellow who sometimes greeted George on the porch of the general store—ambled over, tipping his cap.

"Haven't seen you around in a while, friend," he said. "How's that garden of yours?"

"Well enough," George replied. "Lettuce, onions, carrots doing fine. Might get a decent potato harvest, too."

Burt chuckled. "A man who grows his own. Good. You, uh, mind if I sit a spell?"

"Not at all."

They settled on a log bench overlooking the festivities. The band switched to a slower tune, a gentle melody that drifted across the field. Children chased fireflies in the dim light, their laughter pealing. Burt asked George about fishing conditions, and George, in turn, asked about Burt's farmland. Conversation flowed easily, bridging their drastically different lifestyles.

"Used to do more hunting," Burt mused, "but these knees ain't what they used to be. Miss the hush of the forest sometimes."

George nodded, offering a quiet smile. "The hush is always there if you want it. Just might be a slower walk."

They shared a laugh. Over by a concession stand, a small fuss arose—someone had spilled lemonade all over themselves, provoking gentle ribbing from onlookers. Burt sighed contentedly.

"Ah, I love these fairs. Reminds me how we're all in this together, you know?"

George watched the swirl of people in the glow of lanterns and string lights. "Yes," he said. "It's nice to see everyone celebrating. The year can be hard in these parts. Good to have a reminder we're not alone."

At that, Burt excused himself to check on some friends. George lingered, listening to the music fade in and out. Eventually, Linda waved him over, pressing a paper box of leftover pastries into his hands. "You'll want these tomorrow morning, trust me," she insisted, smiling at his protest. "It's no trouble. Consider it thanks for that painting you gifted me last year—still hanging in my kitchen, you know."

He accepted, touched by her kindness. A hush spread as an announcer took the stage, promising a brief fireworks display to cap the evening. People gathered in small clusters to gaze at the sky. The first rocket whistled upward, exploding in a burst of gold sparks. Oohs and aahs rippled through the crowd. George found a place near some children squealing with delight at each flash of color. He recalled the last time he'd seen fireworks—maybe years ago, perched on the edge of the lake in a canoe, watching reflections glitter on the water. Tonight, the sense of shared wonder was infectious.

With the fireworks done, the fair began winding down. Booths packed up, the band started storing their instruments, and families herded drowsy children toward cars. George recognized the signs—people returning to their daily lives, the ephemeral magic of the fair dissolving until next summer. He gathered his new honey jar, Linda's pastry box, and a few small souvenirs from local artisans. Bidding farewell to Linda and Tim, he made his way to his truck.

The engine grumbled awake. Pulling out of the makeshift lot, he glanced back at the fairgrounds, lights dwindling and people dispersing. He felt a tug of warmth, a subtle gratitude that he'd chosen to attend. While solitude defined him, it was good to see the other side of life—community, tradition, camaraderie. The drive home was peaceful, the sky inky black except for a fat crescent moon that bathed the countryside in pale silver. The roads were quiet, a few headlights flickering in the distance. Cicadas and tree frogs chorused in the ditches as he rumbled past.

When he finally reached his cabin's dirt path, the headlights cut a swath through dense pines. A faint feeling of relief and comfort spread through

George. Home. The hush welcomed him back, though the forest was hardly silent—crickets, owls, and the gentle lap of water formed its own nighttime symphony. He parked, stepped out, and let the night air embrace him. Above, stars glittered. The day's intensity seeped away, leaving him with a sense of fullness and calm.

Inside, he lit a lantern and set his gathered items on the table: honey, pastries, a small carved wooden spoon from Tim's booth. The atmosphere felt sweetly domestic. He brewed a final mug of tea—some wild mint steeped in hot water—and settled into his rocking chair near the window. The lake lay invisible in the darkness, but a breeze from its surface drifted through the open panes, cooling the cabin's interior.

He took a few moments to reflect. The fair had reminded him that life could be lively and communal, people forging connections to support one another. Yet here he was, content to be alone with his thoughts, letting the forest's quiet presence settle around him. He realized both worlds held beauty: the bustle of neighbors chatting, children laughing, pies shared under a blazing sun, and the steady hush of pines and lake that framed his daily routine. One wasn't better than the other—just different. He was thankful he had the freedom to experience both as he pleased.

Picking up his journal, he began scribbling the day's events:

August 15th: Visited the Kincaid Falls Heritage Fair. Warm day, fairgrounds packed. Linda's strawberry-rhubarb pie was splendid. Saw Tim carving spoons, Burt in good spirits. Local band, fireworks at dusk. A welcome glimpse of community—reminds me the town thrives, even if I'm rarely among them. Brought home honey and pastries. Feeling oddly refreshed—like I've stepped briefly into a carnival of human warmth, returning now to nature's hush.

He paused, tapping the pen on the page, remembering the swirl of music and bright colors, children's laughter. Then he added:

Sometimes a man needs solitude to hear his own thoughts, but sometimes he needs neighbors' voices to remember he's part of a larger story. Today felt like both—quiet inside, but touched by others' presence.

Satisfied, he shut the journal. Outside, a barred owl hooted, its call echoing through the night. The lantern's glow cast soft flickers across the log walls, enveloping him in a cozy cocoon. He realized the pastries Linda gave him would be perfect with coffee at dawn, a small reminder of the fair's warmth carried into his next morning.

With a tired sigh, he banked the fire in the stove—though the night wasn't cold, the gentle flame gave the cabin a comforting presence—and slipped into his bunk. Pulling a light blanket over himself, he closed his eyes. The events of the day drifted like a pleasant dream: fiddles playing, sun beating down, neighbors greeting him by name, the sweet taste of pie. All that mingled with the memory of pines and still waters that lay just beyond the cabin walls.

In the hush that followed, George felt an unusual sense of connection to both the wilderness and the people who shared this pocket of the world. The forest might be his constant companion, but it did not stand in opposition to community. In fact, the two coexisted, weaving together the tapestry of life in these parts. The old man with the gray beard who lived at the lake's edge was no hermit cut off from humanity—he was one thread among many, a participant in the ongoing story of Kincaid Falls and the north woods that cradled it.

He drifted into sleep, lulled by the forest's nocturnal lullaby, content in the knowledge that he could step into town's embrace whenever he chose and return to his solitary retreat at will. In that choice lay a rare freedom, and he cherished it deeply. Even as the night wore on, the echoes of fiddles and laughter lingered in his dreams, braided with the soft sigh of wind through pines.

And so concluded the day of the Heritage Fair, bridging solitude and camaraderie, forging a gentle reminder that George was never truly alone in the world. The circle of life in the woods expanded to include the warmth of neighbors, the traditions of a small town, and the shining promise of another morning to come under the endless northern sky.

12

AUTUMN'S BRILLIANT COLORS

A subtle change drifted into the north woods, carried on a cool morning breeze that whispered of autumn. George felt it as he rose from his bunk one early September day, the air in the cabin crisper than it had been even a week ago. Outside, in the gentle glow of dawn, the forest exhaled a hush that only came when summer's chorus began to diminish. He stood on his porch in the half-light, gazing over the lake's surface. Mist curled in ghostly swirls, and the tips of a few maples across the water already glowed with a faint red. Autumn was coming.

He brewed coffee on the woodstove, reluctant to let the chill settle too deep in the cabin. He inhaled the warm steam, reflecting on how swiftly the seasons seemed to shift here—summer had been long and abundant, yet it always ended with an almost imperceptible turn of the cosmic wheel. Before long, the forest would burst into a riot of color, and George welcomed the idea of capturing that moment with his paints and camera, just as he did each year. Outside, a loon's tremolo call echoed, faint but clear, as if greeting the dawn and bidding farewell to summer.

Stepping into the yard, George noticed the morning dew clung heavily to the grass, refracting the sunrise in tiny prisms. He walked down to the lake for a closer look. Along the shore, ferns rustled with the movement of small animals—chipmunks, squirrels, or maybe a fox darting away unseen. In the still air, the lake reflected a rosy sky streaked with gold. The sight filled him with a gentle longing; the transition from one season to another always stirred up both excitement and nostalgia.

By midday, the sun had climbed high, chasing away the chill. Warmth lingered, though less intense than the midsummer heat. George decided it was an ideal day to paddle the shoreline, searching for early signs of color. He gathered a small lunch—bread, cheese, and apples—along with his camera, and slipped the canoe into the water. As he pushed off, the woodsmoke scent from his cabin faded, replaced by the lake's fresh, earthy aroma.

He paddled leisurely, hugging the bank, scanning the trees. Most remained summer-green, but here and there he spotted a sugar maple already tipped in bright orange. A few birches looked paler, as if they'd decided to turn early. Sunlight sifted through the branches, glinting off the water. Below the surface, he glimpsed fish darting in the shallows—small bass, bluegills, perhaps the occasional perch. On a rocky outcrop, a turtle basked in the mild warmth, head raised in silent greeting as George glided past.

By the time he returned, early evening's golden light slanted over the clearing. The air held a subtle coolness again, and the first crickets had begun their evening song. It felt like a promise of things to come: crisp mornings, vivid foliage, and the smoky tang of woodstoves in the air. George, docking the canoe, took a moment to look around. A few geese honked distantly overhead, possibly early migrants testing their flight patterns. He anticipated the coming weeks with quiet joy.

Late summer and early autumn meant harvest time in George's garden. The vegetables he'd nurtured through the warm months now stood ready. Onions dried in small bundles, their stalks browning. Plump carrots peeked from the soil, and bean vines hung heavy with pods. One morning, he rolled up his sleeves and set about gathering a bountiful haul. The ground, damp from a recent rain, yielded carrots easily. He brushed away clumps of dirt, chuckling to himself at the misshapen roots—a testament to nature's unpredictability and the rocky soil near his cabin.

He worked contentedly, placing each vegetable in a woven basket. Sunlight filtered through the pines, warming the back of his neck. A few bright leaves drifted down from a maple overhead, landing among the rows of plants. The forest around him buzzed with late-summer insects, and from the lake came the occasional slap of a beaver's tail or the splash of a fish rising. Over the gentle chatter of nature, George hummed a tune under his breath, feeling accomplished and at peace.

After a couple of hours, he paused to admire the stacked baskets. Onions, carrots, the last of his beans, and a modest crop of potatoes. It would all keep him well-supplied through the autumn months, supplementing any fish or game he might decide to gather. He set the baskets in a shady spot on his porch, then took a moment to wash his hands in a bucket of water. The sight of his harvest brought a surge of gratitude—this tangible reward for a summer's patience and nurturing.

He spent the afternoon preserving some of it. Slicing onions and carrots for pickling, washing and drying potatoes in preparation for storage. The cabin filled with the tang of vinegar as he boiled pickling brine, a scent that mingled with the faint fragrance of pine logs stacked by the stove. When his jars were sealed and cooling on the counter, he felt a calm satisfaction. Autumn's approach might bring shorter days and cooler nights, but it also promised hearty meals and the comforting ritual of putting away provisions for winter.

One of George's favorite autumn traditions was plein air painting amid the vibrant color change. As the days passed, more leaves ignited in tones of gold, crimson, and russet. Even the undergrowth gleamed with amber ferns and orange shrubs, turning the forest floor into a tapestry of warm hues. One crisp morning, he strapped his easel, canvas, and paints onto a small cart behind his truck and drove a short distance to a clearing he knew overlooked the lake.

He parked at the edge of the woods, then carried his supplies down a gentle slope to where a rocky outcrop offered a broad panorama. The view opened onto a valley of mixed hardwoods and conifers, with the lake shimmering in the distance. Overnight temperatures had dropped enough that a slight morning mist still clung to the lower hollows. It would burn off soon, leaving the treetops in brilliant sunshine.

With careful deliberation, George set up his easel and attached a clean canvas. He squeezed out dabs of paint—cadmium red, alizarin crimson, cadmium yellow, burnt sienna, ultramarine blue, and white—readying his palette for the intense autumn palette he planned to capture. A gentle breeze rustled behind him, carrying the faint scent of leaf litter and damp earth.

He began by blocking in the broad shapes with a light sketch in burnt sienna, outlining the rough positions of the ridges, the lake's curve, and the most prominent patches of color. Then, dipping a brush into a mix of reds and yellows, he started layering the foliage. The forest glowed under his bristles. It was never quite the same from one year to the next; sometimes the reds dominated, other times gold prevailed. This season, the hillside seemed to blaze with oranges so radiant it felt almost unreal.

He painted in quiet absorption, occasionally stepping back to check composition. Each brushstroke became a small act of reverence for the land he loved. At intervals, he'd pause, listen to a gust of wind rattling the canopy, or watch a hawk circling overhead, riding the thermals. The day passed in this gentle rhythm, and he broke only for a quick lunch of bread and cheese. By late afternoon, a finished landscape emerged on his canvas—an impression of the forest at the threshold of autumn's peak. He smiled, wiping his brushes, feeling a twinge of satisfaction.

As sunset neared, the clearing glowed in a softer, honeyed light. He packed his materials, careful not to smudge the wet canvas, and headed back. The ride home was serene, the leaves along the road flickering in the dying sun, each tree wearing the season's fiery mantle. That evening, in his cabin, he set the painting near the window, letting the last light highlight its colors. A quiet pride warmed him. He left it to dry, already pondering another location to paint soon.

Autumn also brought changes in the forest's inhabitants. The black bears foraged more actively, seeking to fatten up for winter. George spotted fresh bear scat and torn-up logs where the animals hunted for grubs. One golden evening, he glimpsed a sow and two cubs trundling across a trail. They halted at the sight of him, the cubs scrambling to climb a small pine, while the mother watched warily. George stood still, offering them space. In moments, the sow snorted, turned, and led her cubs away, leaves rustling in their wake.

Deer roamed the clearings more frequently, nibbling at the last of the succulent greenery.

George often found their hoofprints near his garden fence, though he kept it secure enough to deter hungry mouths. Occasionally at dusk, he'd see a stag silhouette against the horizon, new antlers fully formed and ready for the upcoming rut. As the temperature dipped, a sense of urgency quickened in the forest—creatures preparing for the lean months ahead.

Even the Puma, whose tracks he'd found in late summer, left signs of continued presence. Scratches on a tree trunk, a cache of deer bones discovered near a ravine. George felt that faint thrill whenever he suspected the big cat had passed by. One afternoon, while collecting firewood, he found tracks pressed into the soft soil—distinct, large paw prints flanking a deer hoof mark. The signs told a tale of predator and prey weaving through the same woods he called home.

Though caution guided him, he held no real fear. Living in these woods meant accepting the give and take of nature, ensuring he stored food carefully, remained alert during hikes, and respected boundaries. In exchange, he was granted the privilege of witnessing a wild domain few others ever truly experienced.

As autumn deepened, George's pantry and root cellar filled with the fruits of his labor. He needed little from town, but a brief supply run still felt wise. Milk and coffee were running low, and he fancied picking up a bit of flour in case he decided to bake bread on cooler days. So one cool, clear morning, he warmed up his old pickup, the engine sputtering into life. Patches of autumn color flashed by as he drove along the gravel road, the crisp air whipping through his open window.

Kincaid Falls wore an autumnal garb as well—porch planters brimming with mums, leaves piling in gutters, and the smell of woodsmoke drifting from chimneys. The general store's porch creaked under his boots as he entered. Marlene, behind the counter, beamed.

"George! Good to see you. Stocking up for the colder weather?"

He nodded. "Just a few basics. And some coffee beans if you still have that fancy roast."

Marlene chuckled. "You bet. Also, I set aside a small bag of that new blend you liked last time. Thought you might come for it. Anything else? How's the harvest treating you?"

"Got enough vegetables to see me through," he said. "But a bit more flour never hurts. Maybe some sugar, too—I might do some baking."

While she filled his order, George chatted with a local farmer who'd come in for nails. They exchanged remarks about the vibrant foliage and the recent news: a small farm had sold to new owners, the café had introduced a pumpkin pie special, and rumors of a black bear wandering closer to town. George smiled inwardly at that. He knew the bears roamed all around, not just near his cabin. People in town often forgot how seamlessly wildlife moved when the woods were so close.

After loading supplies into his truck, he stopped briefly at Linda's café for a mug of coffee and a slice of warm apple pie—autumn's sweet bounty. Linda updated him on her own garden's harvest, pushing a jar of homemade applesauce into his hands. "Take it," she insisted. "We've got more apples than we can handle this year." Thanking her, he pocketed the jar and headed home, the truck's cab filled with the aroma of apples and fresh coffee beans. The simple generosity of his neighbors left him with a mellow contentment.

As nights turned chillier, George found comfort in stoking his cabin's woodstove at dusk. The crackle of logs and the warm glow of embers created a snug refuge against the creeping cold that settled outside. By lamplight, he'd whittle new fishing lures or tie flies, occasionally pausing to read a worn novel or scribble notes in his journal about the day's observations. The earlier nights made these activities especially cozy, the sense of shelter and solitude heightened by the darkness pressing in around the log walls.

The smell of burning pine mingled with that of a stew simmering on the stove—carrots, onions, potatoes, and a bit of fresh fish if he'd kept one from the lake. The stew's savory fragrance filled the cabin, reminding George of all the hours he'd spent ensuring he had enough wood, enough preserved vegetables, enough knowledge to navigate the coming winter. Even though autumn was his favorite season, it also heralded the harder months ahead. He embraced the ritual of readiness.

Sometimes, over dinner, he'd recall the day's walk or painting session. If the weather had allowed, he might have gone out with his camera to capture the forest's colors at sunset, the red maples glowing against dark evergreens. Other times, he might have ventured deeper into the woods, checking on the Puma's trail camera. Even if it yielded no new images, the mere act of stepping into those hidden glades felt worthwhile—reminding him of how vast the wilderness remained.

Later, by the hearth's final embers, he'd savor a cup of tea or cider, letting his thoughts wander. He might jot a line or two in his journal:

Sept 18th: Colors intensify daily. Painted near the outcrop, capturing a blaze of orange and crimson. Bear sign near the trail—fresh scat. Puma prints faded. The lake's morning mist was glorious, drifting in ribbons. Life slows now, as the forest prepares to rest.

He'd set the journal aside, stifling a small yawn. The hush of the cabin at night was absolute, broken only by the stove's low crackle. Outside, the forest exhaled a different symphony: wind rustling through drying leaves, maybe a barred owl hooting in the distance. Soon, that hush would be replaced by winter's silence—but for now, the rich tapestry of autumn nights held him in a gentle embrace.

By late September, the forest reached its peak in color. Driving wind and occasional rain stripped some trees early, while others seemed to flame brighter with each passing day. George devoted several mornings to painting, choosing different angles around the lake. One day, he set up his easel on a small peninsula that jutted into the water. From there, he captured an image of mirrored foliage in the lake's surface—golds and reds doubled in the still reflection, broken only by the occasional ripple of a fish or drifting leaf.

Another time, he climbed a modest ridge where he'd camped in past years. The climb left him breathless, but the view rewarded him with a sweeping panorama of treetops in every shade of autumn. Even the evergreens looked darker by contrast. He worked swiftly, mindful of shifting light and an encroaching cluster of clouds. The result was a canvas alive with color, though he admitted to himself it never quite matched reality's brilliance. Perhaps no painting truly could, but he was content to try.

People in town began taking "leaf-peeping drives," occasionally passing along the roads near George's cabin, snapping photos or parking by scenic overlooks. More than once, he spotted a family gathered by the lake's edge, marveling at the reflections. He'd wave politely if they saw him, though he never lingered to chat. After all, these woods were his home year-round, not just a spectacle for a day's outing. Still, he appreciated their admiration of the fleeting beauty nature offered.

One afternoon, while tidying his cabin, George heard a faint knock at the door. Visitors were rare, especially without warning. Approaching, he found Linda, her cheeks flushed from the crisp breeze, holding a small basket.

"I hope I'm not intruding," she said, smiling. "I was passing through on a drive to see the colors and thought I'd drop by."

George smiled. "Not at all. Please, come in."

He ushered her into the cabin, where the woodstove's gentle heat permeated. Linda set the basket on the table—it contained fresh apples, a small jar of jam, and a loaf of homemade pumpkin bread.

"Harvest treats," she explained. "Figured you could use some variety after canning and drying all summer."

Touched, George brewed coffee for them both, feeling a mild, pleasant surprise at this gesture. Linda wandered, admiring the paintings he had leaning against the walls. She paused by one of the recent autumn landscapes.

"This is gorgeous," she murmured. "The forest this time of year is always breathtaking, but you captured it so vividly."

George nodded, rubbing the back of his neck. "The colors are a painter's dream, though fleeting."

They chatted easily. Linda spoke of the café's fall menu—pumpkin pies, hearty soups. She mentioned how the local farmers were expecting a sharp freeze soon, urging everyone to gather the last of their produce. George talked about the Puma sightings, though quietly, aware that not everyone relished the notion of a large predator nearby. Linda seemed intrigued but not fearful, nodding thoughtfully.

Before she left, she asked to step onto the porch and view the lake. The air outside was cool, carrying the scent of fallen leaves. She glanced around at the golden canopy and the water shimmering behind it.

"You're lucky," she said softly. "This kind of peace, surrounded by such beauty."

George followed her gaze. "It's a good life," he agreed.

With a final hug of thanks and a wave, Linda departed, her truck rumbling away down the dirt path. George stood watching until the forest reclaimed its hush. A moment of companionship had touched his otherwise solitary day. He returned inside, slicing a piece of the pumpkin bread and savoring its sweetness, a small comfort that lingered.

By early October, the grand display of color began to wane. Gusty winds stripped whole sections of canopy in mere hours, creating drifts of leaves at the forest floor. The lake's edge bristled with fallen branches and debris after each storm. Migrating geese honked overhead in ragged V-formations, sometimes pausing to rest on the water's surface in a flurry of feathers and noise.

George took one last tour with his canoe, paddling amid floating leaves and chilly breezes. He wore a thick flannel now, finding the days cooler and the sun's warmth less penetrating. Still, he enjoyed the rhythmic dip of the paddle, the quiet swirl of water. A few lingering maples still flamed with color, but most of the forest had shifted to a subdued palette of browns, grays, and evergreens. Winter lurked on the horizon.

On the final mild day, he retrieved his fishing net and cleaned it thoroughly, storing it in the cabin loft. The canoe he placed under a makeshift roof extension, propping it upside down on sawhorses to keep snow from piling inside once the flakes began to fall. He checked his firewood supply, stacking fresh cords in neat rows against the cabin's wall. The tang of cut oak and maple filled the air, satisfying in its promise of warmth during the dark months.

In the evenings, the sun set earlier and earlier, often painting the western sky in muted pinks or deep purples that reflected briefly on the lake's calm surface. George stood on his porch sometimes, watching the dim light fade, acutely aware of how each day offered fewer hours of sunlight. The forest's nighttime calls changed, too—fewer insects, more distant owl hoots, and the occasional rustle of a foraging deer. The hush grew deeper.

One twilight, after a particularly blustery day that knocked countless leaves loose, George lit a lantern and sat at his kitchen table. He turned through the pages of his journal, scanning entries from the past weeks: notes on autumn paintings, descriptions of wildlife encounters, the day at the Heritage Fair, Linda's surprise visit. The pages painted a picture of a season bursting with color, harvests, and quiet reflections. He found himself smiling at how seamlessly life had moved from the fullness of summer to the splendor of fall.

He penned a final note for the evening:

October 5th: The woods nearly bare in places. Most color gone, except a few maples clinging to bright leaves. Winter's breath not far off. I can see it in the early morning frosts, feel it in the wind's bite. Harvest is in, preserves stocked. Painted many autumn scenes—might do one last session if the weather holds. Then it's time for winter chores. Each year, autumn leaves me in awe, reminding me how life changes constantly, yet circles back in a grand cycle.

After setting down his pen, he stared at the lantern's flame dancing in the gentle draft. Outside, a gust rattled the windowpane, carrying the scent of freshly fallen leaves. The forest might soon shed its garments, but George felt warmed by the memories of this colorful transition. He banked the stove's fire, ensuring the cabin remained cozy through the night.

Before climbing into his bunk, he stepped onto the porch, breathing in the cool air that hinted of frost. Stars glimmered through the skeletal branches of trees. His breath condensed in faint plumes. In that hush, he sensed the forest settling into the next chapter, the final notes of autumn's song fading gracefully. By tomorrow, more leaves would drift down, carpeting the trails, and soon the land would stand poised for winter's quiet reign.

Yet for now, the beauty of autumn lingered, echoing in his heart. He felt an abiding gratitude for the season's gifts—fiery leaves, abundant harvest, the glow of late-day sunshine on the lake, and gentle moments shared with neighbors. It was enough. Closing the cabin door, he let the darkness envelop the clearing. Tomorrow, the forest would beckon again, and he would greet it with open arms, ready for whatever wonder or challenge lay ahead.

In that moment, this Chapter reached its gentle conclusion: the north woods, in all its brilliant autumn glory, had shown once more how precious and fleeting life's radiance could be. And George, content in his log cabin by the lake, carried that radiance within him—an ember of warmth to sustain him through the cooling nights and the winter soon to come.

13

PREPARATIONS FOR WINTER

A thin surface of ice along the lake's edges greeted George one brisk morning in mid-October, signaling winter's impending arrival. The sun had yet to fully clear the horizon, and the cold bit at his exposed cheeks, nudging him to pull his scarf tighter. Gone were the lingering echoes of summer warmth; autumn's brilliant colors lay scattered and fading on the ground. Most of the trees now stood bare, their branches etched against a pallid sky. Only the evergreens offered a hint of color, their dark needles providing a quiet constancy in a season of change.

George trailed a few paces from his cabin, boots crunching lightly over frosted leaves. In the early light, the forest exhaled a hush, as though holding its breath before the snows arrived. He crouched near the water's edge, studying the narrow band of ice. Thin and brittle, it broke with the slightest tap of his gloved finger, but even this delicate glazing heralded the transition from autumn's final days to the first flirtations of winter. Soon, the entire lake would freeze into a silent mirror, inviting him for ice fishing when the surface grew thick enough to safely hold his weight.

He straightened, noticing his breath plume in the chill air, and let his gaze drift to the stands of birch and pine around him. The morning's hush felt deeper than usual, as if the forest were in the midst of a subtle transformation. He traced the faint tracks of a deer that had ventured to the shoreline, perhaps for a last sip of open water in the night. The sense of a turning page weighed on him, not unpleasantly—every year, he found this cusp between seasons both humbling and invigorating. Winter approached with its hardships, yet also with a certain stark beauty and introspective calm.

Returning to the cabin, he busied himself with the small chores that signaled his readiness for the cold months ahead. He stoked his woodstove, feeling the chill peel away as warmth spread through the log walls. In the broad daylight that gradually filled the cabin, dust motes glimmered and the planks of the floor radiated a gentle glow. Outside, a pair of chickadees fluttered in search of lingering seeds, their fleeting shadows crossing the windows.

George made a pot of coffee, inhaling the rich aroma. As it percolated on the stovetop, he considered the tasks he needed to complete in the coming weeks: stacking more firewood, sealing up drafts in the cabin's corners, checking his supply of kerosene and lantern oil, and ensuring the canoe and fishing gear were fully stowed away. He also wanted to give his winter equipment—particularly his snowshoes and ice auger—a thorough once-over. Winter's invitation would arrive swiftly, and when it did, he aimed to greet it prepared and content.

As soon as the coffee was ready, George drank a cup to chase off the morning chill, then set to work outside. The air felt brisk and clear, and the sun angled low, casting elongated shadows across the clearing. He walked around the cabin, inspecting its exterior for any loose chinking or signs of wear that might cause heat loss during cold spells. The logs held firm; he had sealed them with fresh caulking in the summer. Still, he reinforced a couple of small gaps near the window frames with pliable sealant.

Next, he turned to the roof. While it was older, the cabin's steeply pitched angles allowed snow to slide off more easily. He climbed a sturdy ladder, brush in hand, to clear any accumulated leaves and debris. From his vantage, he glimpsed a wide view of the lake, its surface dancing with early-morning light. Mist still hovered in patches where the water retained residual heat. In the distance, the forest spread across rolling hills, now largely stripped of foliage. A faint wind rustled the pines, carrying a crispness that smelled of dormant earth and distant ice.

After descending, he checked the small shed that housed his generator—a backup for emergencies. The generator itself looked fine, though he made a mental note to change its oil soon. A broken shutter on one side of the shed needed replacement, too. The day's sun rose a little higher, but the temperature remained subdued, never quite shedding that initial frostiness. Still, George appreciated the dryness and clarity of the air. It gave him momentum to complete these chores without the hindrance of rain or slush.

When at last he finished, he paused to survey the yard. The woodpile, stacked neatly over the months, extended along the cabin's north side. He counted at least three cords of split logs, all seasoned and ready to feed the stove. A quiet pride filled him—this tower of wood represented hours of labor but also the promise of a warm interior when the blizzards came roaring across the lake.

In earlier weeks, George had harvested his onions, carrots, potatoes, and late-season beans. Now, his once-lush garden stood mostly barren. The rows of leafy greens had surrendered to cooler nights, and frosted vines draped the low trellis. He scuffed the ground with a boot, turning over a bit of the soil. It smelled rich and dark, prepared to rest beneath the coming snow.

Although the garden was largely done, he spent the next hour uprooting the remaining stalks, adding them to a compost heap along with dried leaves gathered from the clearing. The rhythmic motion of raking soothed him, reminding him of the cyclical nature of his life here—seed, grow, harvest, and return organic matter to the earth to nourish the next planting.

Noting the possibility of an early winter, he resolved to store any leftover produce in his root cellar soon. He already had onions hanging in braided bunches, potatoes tucked in crates, and jars of pickles lining the shelves. Inspecting them, he marveled at how well-prepared he felt for the coming months. Each jar, each crate, each cured onion symbolized self-reliance and the quiet satisfaction of living off the land.

Before heading back inside, George scattered some leftover seeds at the forest's edge for the birds, a small gesture of reciprocity. With the chill intensifying, many migratory species had already departed, but chickadees and nuthatches would remain, gleaning what they could from the dwindling resources.

That afternoon, as George sorted through the last of his summer clothes and set aside heavier flannel shirts, he heard the rumble of a vehicle on the gravel path. Curious, he slipped outside to see Linda's truck pulling up in a swirl of dust and fallen leaves. She hopped out, wearing a warm jacket, cheeks flushed by the crisp air.

"Hope I'm not interrupting," she called, a friendly lilt in her voice. "I was on my way back from picking up supplies and thought I'd drop a few things off."

George couldn't help but smile. Linda had become a more frequent visitor since the fair. Though they'd never define themselves as close friends, a gentle camaraderie had grown between them, nourished by her occasional trips to check on him or to share culinary treats from her café.

He approached the truck, eyebrows lifting at the box she lifted from the passenger seat. "What's all this?"

"Just some extra apples, squash, and flour. Figured you might like them for winter baking—

pumpkin bread, pies, the works." She grinned. "My orchard's still brimming, and the café doesn't need this many."

George took the box, warmth rising in his chest. "That's generous. Let me at least pay you—"

She waved him off. "No need. You can repay me by showing me that latest autumn painting you mentioned."

He chuckled. "Fair enough. Come on in. The cabin's warmer than out here."

Inside, he placed the box on the table, glancing at its contents: a half-dozen squash in varying shapes and colors, a bag of apples, and two large sacks of flour. Enough to fuel many a baking day. Linda peeled off her jacket, rubbed her arms, and cast a curious eye around the cabin.

George fetched a small painting he had started a few days prior—an autumnal scene of the ridge, all aflame with color. Though not quite finished, it captured the vivid interplay of orange, red, and gold leaves under a sky shot with pale clouds. Linda studied it quietly, her expression pensive, then nodded approvingly. "You really bring out the atmosphere. Almost like I can feel that autumn breeze."

They chatted for a while, sipping tea. She inquired about the coming freeze, how he planned to handle the winter. He talked about ice fishing, perhaps a trip into deeper woods for some late-season camping if the conditions allowed. Linda laughed softly at that. "You're braver than me—sleeping outside when the wind cuts. I'd be huddled in a thick blanket by my fireplace with a hot cocoa."

George smiled. "I enjoy the solitude. But I suppose a warm fireplace is nice, too."

Before leaving, Linda handed him a sealed envelope. "A letter from my nephew in the city. He heard about your paintings—he's an art buff. Thought you might want to see it. Maybe he's interested in buying one? Anyway, it's up to you."

George turned the envelope in his hands, intrigued. He rarely sold paintings, preferring to keep them or gift them to friends. But who knew what the nephew might propose? He thanked Linda, and with a wave, she was gone, the truck's engine rumbling down the path again.

Sitting at the table, he opened the envelope and read the brief but enthusiastic note praising the "authentic wilderness landscapes" Linda had described. The nephew invited him to exhibit a painting in a small gallery space he managed in the city. George felt a pang of curiosity tempered by apprehension. Was he prepared to let his art travel beyond the woods? He set the letter aside, mulling it over. For now, winter preparations took precedence, and the city felt far away from his immediate concerns.

Over the next few days, George turned his focus to properly storing all the new supplies Linda had brought, as well as finishing the arrangement of his own harvest. He carried crates of potatoes and apples into the root cellar behind the cabin, placing them on wooden shelves that kept them off the ground. The cellar itself, built partially underground, stayed cool and dark—perfect for preserving produce during the cold months.

He lined up jars of pickled carrots and onions, scanning their seals to ensure everything remained tight. The shelves filled quickly, a testament to the abundant harvest and Linda's generosity. Outside, a stiff breeze rattled the branches overhead. Swirls of dead leaves scurried across the clearing, collecting in small drifts against tree trunks and the cabin's foundation.

Emerging from the cellar, George rubbed his hands together, noticing how the cold air bit deeper each day. The sun sat lower on the horizon now, and its warmest hours felt fleeting. He reckoned that within a fortnight, the first significant snowfall might arrive. Once that happened, his movements in the forest would change—he'd switch from boots to snowshoes, from the canoe to ice fishing gear. The transition never ceased to amaze him, how abruptly the land shifted from autumn's leaf-littered paths to a hushed white expanse.

One late afternoon, deciding to stretch his legs, George ventured along a familiar trail near the ravine. He wanted to see if the Puma's prints or other wildlife signs persisted. A heavy jacket and scarf shielded him from the cutting breeze. The forest exuded a subdued energy—most small creatures hunkered down at dusk to preserve warmth, while birds flew anxiously in search of seeds.

He spotted deer tracks crossing the path, likely a doe and a fawn. Farther on, fresh evidence of a black bear rummaging for the last scraps of nourishment before hibernation: a fallen log torn apart, revealing the tunnel where grubs once lived. He also noticed new scratch marks on a tree trunk about chest height. Could they be from the Puma? Or a bear marking territory? He ran his gloved fingers over the grooves, feeling the raw wood. The forest's watchers still roamed, ever present, even as winter beckoned.

Reaching the ravine's edge, he gazed down. The creek bed carried only a trickle of water, partially iced at the edges. No fresh prints leapt out at him, though a dusting of scattered leaves made tracks difficult to discern. A hush enveloped the spot, tinted with the last dregs of daylight filtering through leafless branches. He recalled the intense moment he'd once locked eyes with the Puma here. A flicker of that primal awe stirred.

As the sun sank, he turned back, mindful that traveling at dusk in near-freezing temperatures demanded caution. Yet, a small spark of gratitude flickered in his chest—this land felt alive and brimming with possibility, even as it retreated into winter's domain. He recognized that each day, each step, offered him the gift of presence in a place where humans were but one species among many.

Though the lake's edges froze and thawed irregularly, George decided to try one last open-water fishing trip before it was sealed for the season. On a clear morning, he found a narrow stretch of shoreline still free of ice. He rummaged out his rod and a small tackle box, more out of nostalgia than necessity—his pantry held plenty of food. Yet the tug of a fish on the line had its own allure, a farewell to open-water fishing until spring returned.

He cast from the bank, letting a spinnerbait flutter in the cold water. The air felt bracing, and the rod stung his fingers whenever a breeze cut across the lake. For a while, nothing stirred. Then, just as he considered packing up, a slight thump traveled up the line. He jerked the rod tip, reeling carefully. The water boiled near the surface, revealing a plump walleye. He played it slowly, mindful that the fish's energy might be sluggish in the chill water. Moments later, he landed it—a decent size, perhaps three pounds. Holding it in gloved hands, he admired the mottled scales and luminous eyes.

Debating whether to release it, he eventually decided to keep it for dinner. He gently ended the fish's struggle and placed it in a small bucket. One fish was enough. Satisfied, he reeled in, noticing how his breath formed small clouds in the frigid air. He took a moment to gaze across the lake—thin ice shimmered along the shore, fractal patterns glinting in the angled sun. Soon, the entire surface would transform, and he'd be drilling holes through ice for his winter catch. With that inevitability on his mind, he trudged back to the cabin to clean the walleye.

The nights grew noticeably longer. By late afternoon, darkness crept through the pines, and the temperature dropped steadily. George made a habit of lighting his lantern shortly after sundown, setting it on the small table by the window. The flickering glow felt comforting, reflecting off the log walls in warm patterns that steadied his thoughts.

He'd sit in his rocking chair, reading an old dog-eared novel or flipping through his journals from past winters. Sometimes he paused to add a new entry about that day's chores or an interesting sighting. After dinner—often a hearty stew or a simple pan-fried fish—he might whittle a small wooden figure, tie new flies for the next year's fishing, or even fiddle with the old radio he kept for rare news updates. The static-laden broadcasts reminded him how distant city life was. He found himself only vaguely curious about the broader world's hustle and bustle.

Now and then, Linda's nephew's letter tugged at his mind. Should he show a painting in a city gallery? The idea felt foreign but not entirely unappealing. He told himself he'd decide after the first snowfall. Perhaps winter's introspection would clarify whether he wanted to share his artwork with a wider audience.

Outside, the forest lay in deepening shadow, the lake's black mirror occasionally reflecting a crescent moon. Owls prowled the silent woods, their calls floating over the treetops. George sometimes opened the door for a moment before bed, breathing in the crisp air, scanning for stars.

The heavens often dazzled him in these cooler months, the Milky Way arcing overhead when the sky was cloudless. Each point of light felt sharper in the cold, as if nature stripped away any haze, revealing the cosmos in stark brilliance.

Shortly after sundown on an especially cold evening, George stepped outside to collect an armful of firewood. The moment he opened the door, he heard a rustling near the woodpile. His senses bristled. In the weak lantern glow cast from the cabin's doorway, he glimpsed a broad silhouette—a black bear rummaging where he'd stacked some extra scraps of fish guts in a sealed container earlier that day.

The bear, clearly hungry, had pried open the container, devouring what remained. It startled at the sudden light, turning its head to stare at George. For a tense instant, man and bear locked eyes. George remained calm; he knew better than to shout or rush forward. Instead, he cleared his throat softly, ensuring the bear acknowledged him.

After a brief moment of indecision, the bear dropped to all fours and ambled away into the dark, leaving a trail of scattered bits. George exhaled slowly. The close proximity reminded him that these creatures, too, were making final preparations before the cold truly descended. He resolved to be more careful with disposal going forward. He'd bury scraps farther from the cabin or burn them when feasible.

He retrieved his firewood, closed the door, and slid the wooden bolt into place. The bear encounter rattled him a bit—he rarely found them so bold this close to the cabin. But hunger and the promise of easy food could override an animal's usual caution. Reflecting on it, he admitted this was nature's territory as much as his. Best to adapt.

One morning, George awoke to find a silver frost coating the windowpanes, delicate crystals forming fern-like patterns in the corners. He dressed quickly, layering thermal undergarments and a thick flannel. Outside, he found the ground dusted with a thin veil of powdery snow—just enough to highlight footprints of small creatures that had crossed the clearing overnight. The air tasted sharper, stinging his nostrils.

He took a brisk walk around the property, leaving boot tracks in the fresh snow. The lake, still mostly open, breathed out a faint mist where cold air met lingering water warmth. In the sky, low clouds scudded by, occasionally dropping tiny snowflakes that vanished upon reaching the ground. Though not a true snowfall, it signaled winter's approach.

Back indoors, he warmed himself by the stove, rubbing numb fingers over the rising heat. He considered how soon the ice might thicken enough for the real winter pursuits—ice fishing, perhaps venturing deeper into the forest on snowshoes. Yet he also felt a pang for the passing year: the kaleidoscope of spring blooms, the lazy warmth of summer afternoons, the brilliant swirl of autumn leaves. Each was gone now, leaving only quiet expectancy for a season of stillness and introspection.

Feeling restless, George gathered his daypack—loaded with a thermos of hot tea, some jerky, and a camera—and set out toward the ravine once more. He wanted to see how the forest looked after the first flurries and whether any more signs of the Puma or other predators were present. The trail, lightly powdered with snow, crunched beneath him. Each step felt deliberate in the hush, like walking through a nearly empty cathedral.

Birches stood stark, white trunks blending with the new snow, while pines and spruces carried a faint dusting on their needles. Now and then, a swirl of wind dislodged snow from the branches, sending a miniature shower drifting to the ground. The subdued color palette—grays, whites, and dark greens—contrasted sharply with the fiery hues of just a few weeks earlier.

At the ravine, the creek had formed thin ice shelves along its edges, water trickling quietly beneath. George crouched, scanning for paw prints. He found older deer tracks, mostly filled in by the dusting. No definite sign of the Puma or bear. A hush enveloped the place, as though the world had paused. He sipped tea, letting the steam warm his face, and remained still for a time, absorbing the scene.

Eventually, a faint motion across the ravine caught his eye—a fox, its red coat muted by the dim light, trotting gracefully along the creek. It halted briefly, ears pricked, perhaps sensing his presence. George stayed silent, heart beating with that old thrill of communion. After a few moments, the fox continued on, weaving through underbrush until it vanished.

He exhaled, a smile forming. Even in the onset of winter, life thrived. The forest might grow quiet, but it never truly slept. In that single fox sighting, he glimpsed the continuity of seasons—the unstoppable dance between creatures and land, each shaping the other.

When George returned, nightfall arrived swiftly. Clouds thickened, and a sharper wind swept over the lake, rattling the cabin's shutters. He placed extra logs in the stove and set a pot of stew to simmer—chunks of squash from Linda's gift, plus onions and carrots from his own stores. The savory smell filled the cabin, blending with the piney tang of burning wood.

Over dinner, he thought about the weeks and months to come: the deeper snows, the hush of the forest, and the possible visits from Linda or an occasional neighbor. He might read more, perhaps respond to that letter from the city. But no matter what, he'd remain attuned to the land's slow pulse under its snowy blanket.

Seated at his small table, lamplight dancing across his journal, he wrote:

October 25th: Light flurries today, frost on the lake's edge. Cabin secured, garden put to bed, wood stacked high. Bear visited the woodpile—reminder to bury scraps further away. Fox sighting near the ravine, no Puma sign. The forest grows still, air biting. Winter stands at the threshold.

He paused, pen hovering, then added:

I'm thankful for autumn's bounty and the community's small kindnesses. As winter draws near, I feel ready—physically and inwardly. The hush beckons.

With that, he set down the pen, banked the stove for the night, and allowed himself a moment of reflection. Outside, the wind's murmur rocked the pines, and tiny grains of snow skittered across the porch. The cabin's interior glowed with a gentle warmth, a sanctuary against the cold's creeping edge.

George blew out the lantern, leaving the embers in the stove to cast a faint orange shimmer on the logs. Crawling into his bunk, he listened to the wind swirl around the eaves, a lullaby for a man who had grown accustomed to nature's rhythms. Sleep soon claimed him, carrying the promise of winter's approach and the comfort of knowing he'd prepared well for the season of cold dark nights.

14

REFLECTION AND GRATITUDE

A silver dawn broke over the lake, the sky tinted with a hushed glow that heralded the season's imminent transformation. George awoke under a thick wool blanket, feeling the nip of winter's breath at the edges of his small cabin. Overnight, the temperature had dropped well below freezing, and when he swung his legs out of bed, the floor felt frigid beneath his socks. He took a moment to pull on an extra sweater and rub warmth into his arms. Outside, in the early light, the pine boughs sagged under a delicate dusting of snow, while the lake's edges had solidified further, turning the shallows into a crystalline shelf.

He stoked the woodstove, stirring the coals to life and adding fresh kindling and logs. Familiar pops and hisses ensued, small sparks dancing behind the stove's grate. Within minutes, a radiant heat filled the cabin, coaxing George into motion. As he waited for the embers to grow into a steady flame, he brewed a pot of coffee and gazed at the frost-laced windows, appreciating the intricacy of the fern-like crystals etched by the night's cold. It was late October, and winter was no longer a distant possibility—it was here, pressing at the threshold.

With the stove now crackling merrily, he poured his coffee, cradling the mug in both hands. Taking his first sip, he closed his eyes, letting that first surge of warmth spread through him. This would be the first real day of freezing temperatures, a sign that the lake might soon lock itself in ice for the coming months. For George, such days always brought a quiet mix of anticipation and introspection. He felt that sense of completion—he had prepared well, the cabin was snug, the pantry stocked, the woodpile ample. And yet he also felt the forest's shifting mood, the hush that settled over pine and birch as the world braced for a season of white.

Once dressed, George ventured onto the porch to breathe the morning air. Thin ice clung to each puddle, and a fine layer of snow coated the path leading to the lake. He noticed how the garden rows, now empty and blanketed in frost, seemed to hibernate as well, stripped of the life that once buzzed among them. Lifting his gaze to the lake, he spotted wisps of fog drifting over the open water at its center. Closer to shore, the ice crust gleamed in pale sunlight. The sight felt bittersweet, a final farewell to the fiery autumn just passed.

He remembered how brilliant the trees had looked, and how only a handful of weeks prior, he could still paddle across the water at dusk. Now, the canoe rested upside down under its shelter, unlikely to move until the thaw. The forest, too, had entered another phase—bare trunks, silent undergrowth, only the occasional evergreen standing dark against the snow. In a month's time, the drifts would be too high for normal walking, and he'd strap on snowshoes to explore the woods.

With a faint smile, he turned to look at the pile of logs stacked against the cabin wall. He'd hauled many of these himself, chopped and split them over the summer, sweating under a blazing sun. Now, each piece promised a cozy night by the fire. If there was any blessing in winter's austerity, it was the clarity it brought. The forest's clamor muted, leaving room for a deeper introspection.

Returning indoors, George finished his coffee and tidied up, then set to a few small tasks. First, he retrieved his snowshoes from the wall hooks, checking their bindings. Though it might be another week or two before enough snow fell to warrant using them, he liked to be ready. A small tear in the rawhide lacing caught his eye. He located his repair kit—a needle, waxed thread, extra strips of hide—and carefully stitched the lacing back together. In the cabin's stillness, the only sounds were the soft hiss of the stove and the faint scratch of his needle through the rawhide.

Next, he moved on to his ice auger, stored in a corner near the door. The steel blade needed sharpening after last season's use. With methodical strokes of a whetstone, he restored its keen edge, occasionally testing the metal's bite by brushing a fingertip against it. The work felt comforting, almost meditative. Each tool he readied represented the coming rhythm of winter: ice fishing trips, treks across frozen lakes, the exhilaration of drilling holes through thick ice to find trout or walleye lurking beneath.

While he worked, the cabin's warmth enveloped him, fending off the chill that pressed against the windows. It was a tiny fortress of wood and logs, standing firm in the silent wilderness. After finishing the auger's blade, George glanced at the old pocket watch on the mantel—still early, yet the sun's angle suggested a short day ahead. He decided to step outside for a brief walk, to see how the woods looked under this fresh, thin layer of snow.

He donned a heavier coat and gloves, then ventured out once more. The clearing around the cabin stretched in a patchwork of frosted grasses and low shrubs, all powdered in white. Each step crunched softly, leaving footprints that broke the pristine surface. A quiet pleasure stirred in him at being the first to walk upon this new snowfall.

He followed a trail that wound through a stand of spruce and hemlock, the denser canopy sheltering the ground so that only a light dusting had reached the needles below. Birdsong was sparse; most migratory species had gone, leaving behind only the hardiest year-round inhabitants. Chickadees flitted from branch to branch, calling faintly. A red squirrel scolded him from atop a log, its bushy tail flicking. But the forest felt otherwise hushed, as if waiting for the deep snows to fully arrive.

Near a small stream that cut through the trees, he paused to peer at icy tendrils forming along the bank. The water gurgled softly, not yet frozen over. He saw a single set of fresh tracks crossing the narrow log bridge—a deer, perhaps, or maybe a fox. Kneeling, George tested the trickle with a bare hand. The cold stung, but he savored the vitality of it. So many animals would soon rely on streams like this for any liquid water once the lakes were frozen solid.

He pressed on until he reached a gentle rise that offered a glimpse of the lake. From that vantage, the water's far side was still open, glinting under pale sunlight, while the closer shore sat shrouded in ice. Though the snow remained scant, a heavier fall could arrive any day. The breeze stiffened, reminding him not to linger too long in one place. But before turning back, he closed his eyes to let the forest's calm seep into him.

Trudging back to the cabin, he reflected on the changing year—how swiftly nature flowed from season to season. In his mind's eye, he revisited the bright chaos of spring blooms, the shimmering green canopy of summer, the blaze of autumn leaves, and now this muted, monochrome approach to winter. Each phase brought its own delights and challenges. This sense of cyclical transformation felt like an anchor, teaching him to adapt, to accept, to find beauty in every stage.

He recalled the high summer days spent fishing, the bull Moose sightings, the black bear rummaging near his woodpile, the glimpses of a Puma that roamed silently through the deep forest. Linda's visits, the heritage fair, the paintings he'd created in a flush of autumn color. All these moments seemed to converge in the quiet hush that was settling now, reminding him that a year in the woods was never truly solitary, never lacking in marvels or companionship.

At the cabin's threshold, he noticed a tiny drift forming against the door. He kicked it aside gently and stepped in, stamping snow from his boots. The stove's heat enveloped him once more, a welcoming embrace against the crisp outdoors. He removed his coat and gloves, setting them to dry near the hearth. Every breath of warm air felt especially comforting now, signifying he had done his due diligence in preparing for winter's challenges.

Over a light lunch—leftover stew warmed on the stovetop—George considered the events of the past months. He thought about writing a letter back to Linda's nephew in the city. Perhaps he'd include a photo of one of his finished paintings, let the nephew decide if it belonged in some gallery exhibition. A part of George felt uncertain. The idea of his artwork leaving these woods to be showcased under artificial lights in a busy city seemed odd. Yet another part of him recognized that art was meant to be shared, that others might find solace or wonder in his depictions of the forest's quiet beauty.

After he finished eating, he fetched his journal, sinking into his rocking chair. Snow-laced light filtered through the windows, softly illuminating the pages. He opened to the most recent entry, scanning his notes on the first ice forming at the lake's edge. Then he turned to a blank page and set pen to paper:

October 30th: The morning brought our first real freeze and a dusting of snow. Lake edges iced over. I've readied my tools—auger, snowshoes, warm clothes. The forest grows silent, animals preparing to outlast the cold. In this hush, I recall the year's bounty: spring's fresh blooms, summer's fishing mornings, autumn's blaze of color, and glimpses of the Puma—wild grace incarnate.

He paused, pen hovering, thinking of how best to capture the season's essence. Then he continued:

I feel a deep contentment, knowing I've done what's needed to welcome winter. The cabin is stocked, and my heart is steady. Each day offers a quiet wonder, even in the starkness of early snow. I might write to Linda's nephew—maybe let one painting find a new audience. Time will tell.

Setting the pen aside, he stared at the final lines. Indeed, time would tell. No need to rush decisions. The winter months stretched ahead, providing ample room for reflection. If he chose to send a painting to that gallery, it could happen once the lake froze solid, and he could more easily make the trip to town. For now, he felt no hurry, only a sense of gentle progression.

The afternoon sunlight remained pale but bright. Determined to complete one last check of the cabin's exterior before nightfall, George stepped outside again. He circled the log walls, ensuring shutters were secure, the chimney clear, and the woodpile covered to keep the snow off. Occasional gusts sent spirals of white dancing across the clearing.

As he rounded the cabin's corner, a movement caught his eye—something small scurrying through the thin layer of snow near the treeline. He recognized the bushy tail and pointed ears of a red Fox. It glanced his way, body tense. For a heartbeat, they regarded each other across the silent white expanse. Then, with a flick of its tail, the Fox dashed off, leaving tiny paw prints in the snow. A smile touched George's lips at the fleeting encounter. Even when the forest felt dormant, life continued in subtle pockets of activity.

He returned inside, mind flickering with gratitude for these small moments of connection. In the hush of winter's first approach, even a simple fox sighting reminded him how the land thrived under the surface, each creature following ancient instincts to survive.

That evening, George treated himself to a special supper. He pulled a jar of pickled onions from the pantry, grabbed a small squash from Linda's gift box, and set about creating a hearty dish. Sautéing onions, garlic, and cubed squash, he added a bit of dried thyme and rosemary, letting the fragrant steam rise in the cabin. The savory smell mingled with the woodsmoke that gently curled from the stovepipe.

While the stew simmered, he rummaged for a loaf of bread he'd baked a few days prior—coarse and crusty, perfect for sopping up stew broth. Outside, dusk fell swiftly, transforming the sparse snow into a glowing landscape under the faint moonlight. He lit the lantern, letting its golden glow fill the cabin's snug interior. The dancing shadows on the walls conjured memories of evenings past, each winter stacking upon the last.

When the meal was ready, he ladled the stew into a deep bowl, carrying it to the small table near the hearth. The first spoonful flooded his mouth with warmth and flavor, a testament to the harvest he'd gathered and the care Linda showed by sharing her squash. As he ate, he felt deeply thankful—for the land that sustained him, for the neighbors who offered kindness, for the slow, cyclical march of seasons that shaped his life in these woods.

After dinner, he cleaned his dishes in a basin of heated water, dried them meticulously, and set them aside. The cabin's coziness seemed amplified by the early nightfall. He added another log to the stove, sparks flying briefly as fresh wood touched the embers. The temperature outside plummeted, but inside, the radiant glow made the air comfortable, almost luxurious compared to the biting cold just beyond the threshold.

He thought about the year's journey—how each chapter of life in the woods had offered its own distinct flavor. From winter's quiet introspection, he'd witnessed spring's exuberant bloom. Summer had brought fishing expeditions, painting sessions by sunlit shores, and new connections in town. Autumn had arrived in a blaze of color, culminating in a harvest of vegetables and rich experiences. And now here he was, at winter's doorstep once more, the circle complete yet ever-renewing.

Stepping outside briefly to gather more wood, he paused to stare at the sky. The moon hung low and bright, illuminating the snowy clearing. A faint shimmer radiated from the lake's surface, where ice and water intermixed. Stars speckled the clear heavens. The air felt so still that he almost imagined he could hear the slow, methodical creaking of the expanding ice along the shoreline.

A subtle satisfaction filled him—this was home, this place of stark beauty and honest labor, of solitude and quiet companionship with nature's creatures. In the silence, he sensed not loneliness but profound connectedness, as if the forest itself acknowledged his presence just as he acknowledged its majesty.

Inside, he placed the extra logs beside the stove, closed and latched the door against the night's chill, and lit a single candle on the windowsill. The lantern's glow mingled with the candle's flicker. He'd learned to appreciate these small sources of light in a dark world. Each flame stood for warmth, hope, and the enduring spirit of life amid winter's dominion.

Setting himself in the rocking chair, he opened his journal for what felt like a concluding entry to the season. The pen's nib touched the paper, and words flowed:

October 31st: Winter arrives with quiet insistence. Snow dusts the land, the lake's edges freeze, and I've readied my tools. Tonight, the sky brims with stars, the moon revealing a hushed world of ice and possibility. Looking back on the year—its seasons, its gifts, its challenges—I feel a deep gratitude. Solitude has not been lonely but enriching. Each encounter with the forest's creatures, each moment painting or fishing, each neighborly exchange—these shaped me, weaving a tapestry of belonging. Now, as snow accumulates, I embrace winter's call. There's comfort in knowing the land sleeps under a blanket of white, and in time, spring will awaken it anew. For now, I rest in the stillness, at peace.

He lingered over the page, re-reading those lines, feeling them resonate with everything that had transpired. Then, with a contented sigh, he closed the journal. Through the window, moonlight illuminated the pines, highlighting their frosty boughs. The cabin's interior glowed softly, the stove popping as another log caught flame.

Before turning in for the night, George set a kettle of water on the stove, brewing a final cup of tea. He sipped it near the embers, the warmth threading through him. Flashes of memory flickered: The Puma's silent grace in the ravine, Linda's spontaneous visits bearing produce, the bull Moose he'd observed in spring, the calm after a thunderstorm on a fishing trip, the swirl of fiery autumn leaves, and the bear rummaging at dusk.

These images felt like living brushstrokes in the year's grand mural.

He also recalled the community bonds, small yet significant—a trip to the heritage fair, Tim's carving demonstration, Marlene's general store, the occasional note or letter connecting him to a wider world. Though he lived at the edge of the wilderness, he was never truly alone. The land, the animals, and the kind people in Kincaid Falls all formed threads of a tapestry that encircled his life.

In the calm that preceded winter's heavier snows, he felt a certainty that he had chosen a path aligned with his soul. Each morning, the forest greeted him with quiet revelations; each evening, the cabin's hearth offered gentle closure. There were challenges—extreme cold, isolation, the need for self-reliance—but they honed his appreciation for life's essentials: warmth, nourishment, and genuine connection.

Finishing his tea, he quenched the candle's flame and banked the stove for the night. Then, with the lantern still burning low, he made his way to the bunk, the floor creaking underfoot. The downy blankets welcomed him, enveloping him in a well-earned sense of comfort. Outside, the wind carried a faint howl across the treetops, and snow grains tapped lightly at the window.

He lay there, listening to the forest's lullaby—wind, branches, the hush of new snow settling. The final chapter of the year closed around him with gentle finality, each season's memories etched in his heart. Tomorrow might reveal deeper snow or new wonders in the tracks of winter animals. In the spring, the cycle would begin anew, buds breaking through the thawed earth, the lake shifting from ice to open water.

But for now, in this moment, he accepted winter's silent invitation. Gratitude filled him—gratitude for the land and its creatures, for a cabin that shielded him from storms, for neighbors who kept him tethered to community, and for the simple joy of living in harmony with nature's cadence. The lantern's light, flickering faintly, cast the final glow of the day upon the walls. Then George closed his eyes, letting sleep rise gently like the tide.

In the darkness, the stove's embers pulsed with life, echoing the steady beat of the forest outside. A fresh chapter of winter awaited. But this night, as he drifted into dreams, all was exactly as it should be: a man at peace with the woods, wrapped in the warmth of a life well-lived, a life in the woods.

The End

ABOUT THE AUTHOR

Blair Edward Russell (B.E. Russell) was born in 1979 in Etobicoke, Ontario, just outside of Toronto. Summers were a blur of outdoor activities—roaming forests, wading through creeks in search of fish, and skateboarding around the neighborhood. After finishing high school, Blair pursued his education at York University in Toronto, graduating in 2007. Not long after, he embarked on a new adventure, relocating to Miami, Florida, with his wife, Ginna, to build their life together in the Sunshine State.

Blair's creativity doesn't stop at writing. He's also an avid oil painter, a domain name investor, and an accomplished internet entrepreneur. Most of all, he's a passionate angler, especially when it comes to fly fishing. He writes many types of novels—including Epic Fantasy Adventures, Light Horror, Mysterious Tales, and novels about the Outdoors—drawing heavily on his love of fishing to craft stories that hook readers and take them on thrilling, unforgettable journeys.

Today, Blair lives in South Florida with his wife Ginna. Whether he's crafting a new original tale, painting in his studio, or casting a line into tranquil waters, Blair finds inspiration in life's simple yet extraordinary moments.

ACKNOWLEDGEMENTS

I would like to thank the following people who have helped inspire me and supported me throughout my life in all the various projects and endeavors I have been through.

My wife Ginna, My father and mother Bob and Marie, My brother and sister Bobby and Stacey, all of my friends and extended family as well as you my passionate reader.

You are all the ones who inspire me to share my dreams and ideas with the world.

FURTHER READING

Please be sure to check out the other fine books from **B.E. Russell** including:

- *Trial by Fire*
- *Emberheart*
- *Stories from the Grave – BOOK ONE*

If you enjoyed reading this novel be sure to join my mailing list at www.BlairEdwardRussell.com. And check in on my website often to find information on my latest novels.